TRAINER

AN MC ROMANCE (OUTLAW SOULS BOOK 3)

HOPE STONE

© Copyright 2020 - All rights reserved.

It is not legal to reproduce, duplicate, or transmit any part of this document in either electronic means or in printed format. Recording of this publication is strictly prohibited and any storage of this document is not allowed unless with written permission from the publisher except for the use of brief quotations in a book review.

This book is a work of fiction. Any resemblance to persons, living or dead, or places, events or locations is purely coincidental.

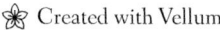 Created with Vellum

DEDICATION

This book is dedicated to YOU, the readers and supporters of indie authors like myself. Your posts and kind words on Facebook and Email give me the motivation to keep writing and publishing these stories for you all. Thank you!

Now prepare to escape into the world of The Outlaw Souls MC!

Ready to meet Trainer?...

ONE
TRAINER

There was nothing in the world, quite like riding a bike. I lived for it. Every time I threw my leg over a motorcycle, a tingle of excitement gathered in the base of my spine. It was freedom, rebellion, and fun all rolled into one.

I'd discovered my passion for the ride when I was only sixteen years old. Back then, I'd been desperate for a car, as anyone is at that age. I thought it would impress the ladies, not that I knew a damn thing about women.

As a foster kid that bounced around the system for years, I'd known that I was on my own when it came to vehicle purchases. No foster parent I'd met would ever dream of buying me one, if they could even afford to at all.

So, I scrimped and saved, working in the dish room of a cafe after school and on the weekends for as many hours as I was legally allowed. After three months, I was ready. I searched the classifieds in the newspaper for the perfect car, but instead, I stumbled across an ad for a used motorcycle. I called up the guy selling it and set up a time to take a look at it, to satisfy my curiosity. Once I set my eyes on that cherry red and chrome machine, I was in love. It was a Honda 250, so not exactly a powerful bike, but it had some get-up-and-go. It didn't get up to a high enough speed for the highway, but it was fun to ride around town. It was my primary mode of transportation for two years before upgrading to my first Harley-Davidson, which was the bike I had when I joined the Outlaw Souls.

Outlaw Souls was the motorcycle club that I'd been involved with for the past ten years. We were a brotherhood.

Motorcycles were a huge part of my life. I rode them for fun and fixed them up for a living. Buying classics and restoring them to resell was a lucrative way of earning income. And I'd heard it said that if you love what you do, you'll never work a day in your life. I wasn't sure if I bought into that, but I knew that I wasn't suited for working in an office or anything like that.

"Damn, that thing is a beauty," Ryder, our MC president, let out a low whistle as I pulled up beside him, straddling my most recent restoration.

I smirked. "You're looking at a '77 XLCR."

"Nice Cafe Racer," Pin, our treasurer, said as he wandered over to us.

We were meeting in the parking lot of The Blue Dog Saloon. The bar was owned by Yoda, our Chaplain. His brother, Padre, used to be our president, until things went south a couple of years back, ending in Padre's untimely death and Ryder taking up the responsibility of leading us. We were all unsure about how Yoda would take the transition, losing his brother in a bloody confrontation like that, but Ryder somehow smoothed it all over. It was a private matter, so I wasn't sure how that went down, but it must have been one hell of a conversation. After all, it was Ryder that killed Padre. He didn't set out to do it, but he didn't have much choice.

The whole thing was a mess, and it had shaken things up, as expected, but there was peace in the club now. Ryder had stepped into the role of leader with a plan to shift the focus of the Outlaw Souls from escalating violence and illegal activities that plagued La Playa to trying to protect the community from such things. This was our home, after all.

We weren't saints by any means, still involved with arms dealing and not afraid to break the law when we felt it was necessary, but we made sure not to do that locally. This town had enough problems from our rivals, Las Balas. Their sex trafficking and drug running was out of control, a real plague on the area.

I lowered the kickstand of the bike, stepping off as I killed the engine. This motorcycle was much lighter than my normal ride, which was one of the many unique characteristics of this particular model. It was also a slim bike with a long wheelbase and a bikini fairing. The look alone was the reason it was a collector's item.

I pulled the black helmet off my head, placing it on the seat. I didn't have to worry about securing the thing. No one was going to walk off with my helmet, or *any* of my property for that matter in Outlaw Souls' territory. Besides, we always assigned a Prospect to watch over the motorcycles so that they were never unattended. Our prospective members had to do things like this to prove themselves worthy before becoming Patches - which was what we called our official club members.

There were currently ten Patches and three Prospects, but we were always a growing organization. The ride I had scheduled for us today included the entire club as well as more casual bikers from the community, making a total of 28 people. It was a good opportunity for locals to get to know the Outlaw Souls, to erase any stigma from the activities of clubs like Las Balas. We might even get a few new Prospects out of it.

As Road Captain, it was my job to organize the rides, planning routes, and making sure that everyone followed the rules. As I walked into the bar, all eyes were on me. Usually, Ryder led all meetings, but these rides were my responsibility. So, I remained standing while everyone around me sat, with my hip leaning against the brass railing along the wooden bar, and my arms crossed over my chest.

I launched into a speech that was well-worn after many years, so I hardly had to think about what I was saying anymore. It was always the same. I covered the length of the ride and the stops we would make to rest. Some people preferred the spontaneity that lack of planning offered, but my first priority was safety, which required developing a strategy and sticking to it. We would be riding in formation the entire time, with Ryder leading the way. I would be second, followed by the least experienced riders. It was better to put those people in front of the pros, so that they could be watched. The last thing I wanted was to leave someone behind because they couldn't keep up. I assigned Swole to ride in the back, making her the sweep rider that set the pace.

All the Outlaw Souls had heard this a million times before, but they listened silently, giving me the respect of their undivided attention. It was a sign of my efficiency as a Road Captain and the importance of the position I held.

Finally, I reminded everyone that we didn't want showboats in the group. No competing or going rogue. This wasn't about showing off. These rides were about the entire group moving as one. We were a brotherhood on the road, even when we were riding with non-members like today.

We headed out after that. I double-checked that the first aid kit was in one of my leather saddlebags. The other one held a few basic tools, just in case there were any mechanical malfunctions on the road. The MC members all kept their bikes in pristine condition, so it had never happened before, but I believed in being prepared. Pin liked to tease me about being a boy scout in a past life, because I sure as hell wasn't one in this one.

We all mounted our bikes and fired them up, the roar deafening. Ryder and I nodded to one another before pointing our bikes south. Then, we were off on a ride through the winding back roads of southern California, with the bright sun shining overhead as we left La Playa behind for the afternoon.

TWO
ERICA

"Are we there yet?"

I sighed through my nose before forcing a smile onto my face as I met my son's eyes in the rearview mirror. It was the third time he'd asked in the last hour, but I knew it wasn't fair to get irritated with him. We'd been on the road for almost eight hours now, and I was more than ready to arrive at our destination myself.

"Almost, buddy," I glanced down at the GPS on my phone, which claimed that we would reach La Playa in half an hour.

Dominic didn't respond, just turning to look out the window, watching as we passed a huge apricot orchard. The scenery had been lovely as we traveled west across Arizona and Southern California. There was a lot of flat farmland as well as green, rolling hills. Now that we were going North, I could see a mountain range in the distance, providing a stunning backdrop on such a bright, spring day.

A loud rumbling sound drew my attention, making me frown. *What is that?*

My silent question was answered as I rounded a

curve, and I saw dozens of motorcycles heading my way. My eyes widened as I took the sight in. There were men and even a few women wearing leather jackets and helmets as they straddled their bikes. They all seemed to move in unison as they took a sharp corner, their machines leaning to the left before straightening out. Everyone I saw was wearing a pair of dark sunglasses as well, which I figured came in handy on bright days. They didn't exactly have visors they could use to block the harsh rays of the sun.

As the group passed my small Toyota, I could feel the vibrations from their powerful engines in the center of my chest. I forced my eyes to stay forward, paying attention to the road ahead. The last thing I needed right now was to wreck my car because I was gawking at a bunch of bikers. It wouldn't help me to stay under the radar, and that was exactly what I had to do right now. Another glance in the rearview mirror showed that Dominic was waving at the bikers as we passed. Most of them were returning the gesture.

Thirty-two minutes later, I pulled up to the curb in front of a two-story duplex. I swallowed thickly as my eyes traveled over our new home. An unexpected emotion clogged my throat as I couldn't help measuring this place against the house that I left this morning.

There was no comparison. This duplex was nothing like the five-bedroom estate I called home for the past eight years. That house had been built to our specifications and meticulously maintained. My husband, Jeff, was very concerned with appearances. So, he spared no expense, ensuring that we lived in luxury. The place was bigger than we needed, even after Dominic was born, but I'd be lying if I said that I didn't love the house. It was gorgeous.

It was also the place that my life turned into a nightmare.

I shook my head at my conflicting thoughts. The house in front of me might not be fancy, but it was *mine* and mine alone. I would be safe here.

Who cared if the siding needed a good power washing or the concrete steps leading up to the porch looked like they might crumble under our feet? The surrounding houses also looked a little rough, so I surmised this might not be the best neighborhood, but I was going to make this work.

"Mom, is this where we're going to live now?"

I put the car in park and unbuckled my seatbelt so that I could turn and look at Dominic. His expression showed no distaste as he stared at the house, just quiet regard. I wished that I had his innocent curiosity. It would be so much better than dwelling on the negative aspects of my situation.

"It sure is," I said, hoping that he couldn't hear the strain in my happy-go-lucky tone. "This'll be our new home."

Dominic turned to look at me, and I was struck by the haunted look that lingered in his eyes. He'd seen so much darkness in his seven years of life.

That strengthened my reserve. I was doing the right thing here. Our house back in Arizona might have been big and beautiful, but that was just for show. What mattered was the life that was lived on the inside, and I was going to do everything within my power to ensure that Dominic was happy here. I couldn't remember the last time he'd smiled easily or slept through the night without nightmares, and I was desperate to restore that part of life for my little boy. He deserved a better childhood.

"Let's go in and check it out," I said, stepping out of the car.

I pulled open the back door of the car and helped Dominic out of his booster seat, nearly bumping my head on the top of the door frame. I wasn't used to this small car yet, as I had purchased it this morning, using cash that I had been squirreling away for months. My roomy SUV was bought brand new six months ago, but it was in my husband's name. I couldn't take off in that, since it would be too easy to track down. The thing that made this place safe was that Jeff had no idea where we were. I wasn't sure what he'd do if he tracked me down, but he was a violent man.

I knew that I had to carefully consider everything once I decided to leave. Jeff would definitely try to find me. Not because he cared about me, but because he considered me his property, and his massive pride wouldn't allow me to leave without a fight. That was all our marriage was - one big fight.

The only good thing to come out of it was my little boy. I held Dominic's hand as we walked up the concrete path to the porch. To my relief, the porch steps were sturdier than they looked. The porch itself was divided in half, a low wall separating two front doors. The house was split into two separate dwellings, sharing only a front and back yard. I knew that a family already lived in number twenty-one, but I hadn't met them yet. In fact, I hadn't even seen this property in person before I put down a deposit. Desperation led me to take the first thing that I could find, hoping that the pictures online weren't deceiving in any way.

I reached into the mailbox of number nineteen and pulled out a silver key, right where the landlord had promised it would be. Unlocking the door, I held my breath as I pushed it open and got my first look at the place.

The first thing that caught my eye was the dark hardwood floor. It was a little scratched up, but I liked it all the same. We were in the living room, and directly ahead, I could see a small dining room. There were french doors separating the two rooms. Two panes of glass were missing, but I like that the woodwork looked original to the house, matching the frames of the large windows and the banister of the stairs to my left.

I felt tension ease out of my shoulders as I exhaled. This wasn't that bad. It had a certain charm to it that made people fall in love with older homes. As I shut the door behind us, Dominic headed toward the stairs. They creaked as he tentatively walked up the first few steps.

"Why don't you go on up and pick your room while I check out the kitchen?" I suggested. I knew from talking to the landlord that there were two bedrooms upstairs of roughly the same size, so it really didn't matter to me which one I ended up with. I just hoped that this would help Dominic to feel like he had a little control over his own life.

I walked into the kitchen, and my eyebrows popped up in surprise. The only picture online of this room had shown the stove and countertop, so I had no idea that the walls were covered in seventies-style wood paneling. Combined with the dark wood cabinets and black appliances, I felt like I had just walked into a cave.

A tacky, outdated cave.

"Yikes," I mumbled.

At that moment, I heard a siren outside. Returning to the living room, I glanced out the window just in time to see two police cars go speeding by. I worried my bottom lip, wondering if they were heading somewhere nearby.

"You okay, mom?" Dominic's voice came from right behind me, making me jump as I spun around.

"Uh... yep. I'm perfectly fine."

Squatting down in front of him, I reached out and

brushed his thick brown hair off of his forehead. He needed a haircut.

"Then, can we have pizza for dinner?" he asked, not seeming to notice as a third police vehicle went by.

I smiled. This boy could eat pepperoni pizza every day of his life if I'd let him. "Sure. Go get your jacket."

It might be springtime, but this was a coastal town, and I was willing to bet that the spring evenings could get a little chilly with the wind coming in off the water. Dominic was quick to obey.

When we returned after dinner at a Pizza franchise I was familiar with, I unpacked the car, which was full to bursting with everything that we now owned. I didn't have time or space in the car to take everything that I would have liked. When Jeff left for work this morning, I had gone through the house, shoving clothing and other valuables into duffle bags and suitcases. I had reduced my entire world to whatever I could fit in the back of a Toyota Corolla. We didn't even have furniture and would be using air mattresses for a couple of nights until I could have beds delivered.

I made a mental note to get that taken care of as soon as possible. But first things first, I needed to find a job somewhere in this town.

Later, after Dominic had gone to bed, I went into our new bathroom with a box of Chestnut Brown hair dye. The harsh chemical smell made me wrinkle my nose, but I applied the dark goop liberally onto my flaming red hair. Living on the down-low meant that I had to cover up my most distinguishing feature. My scalp was tingling by the time the ten-minute treatment was complete. When I rinsed the dye from my hair, I barely recognized the person staring back at me.

Somehow the darkness of my hair made my skin look

even paler. Opening up a plastic container that encased a brand new pair of scissors, I gathered the bulk of my long hair in one hand and made the straightest cut across that I could manage, so that my waves rested on the tops of my shoulders.

I smiled at my reflection. Change could be a good thing, and I was going to embrace this one. Tomorrow was going to be a new beginning.

TWO DAYS LATER, I still hadn't found a job, and it was shocking how much I had depleted my stash of cash. I hadn't had to worry about money for such a long time, since well before I married Jeff, and it didn't occur to me how expensive everything would be. I tried to be sensible about purchases, buying gently used furniture, and avoiding name-brand food when stocking the refrigerator and pantry, but I was still going to be broke before the end of the month if I didn't find a source of income immediately.

Jeff's taunting words seemed to echo in my head as I got back into my car after a disastrous job interview. *"You can't leave. You're worthless. You'll never make it on your own. You need me."*

How many times had I heard some version of those words come out of his mouth? He had been trying to break me down emotionally, but I always held onto the belief that he was wrong. Now, I had to wonder... was he *right*?

One of the problems I was having was that I didn't have identification. Well, none that I could use. I needed to be paid under the table for now, until I could find a person in this town that made fake IDs. Paying income tax with my real name would be the same as sending Jeff a postcard with my new address written on it. He had resources and money for the best private investigators. I had to stay on my toes to avoid their detection.

The other problem I was running into was that I had no job skills. Jeff was born with a silver spoon in his mouth, inheriting his position on the Board of Directors at the family company. I often wondered if being a trust-fund-baby led him to behave the way that he did. Growing up so spoiled like that must affect someone's personality. Still, he had more than enough money, and there was no need for me to work. Over time, as Dominic got older, I had toyed with the idea of doing it anyway, just to give myself something - anything - outside of the house that I could call my own. But he was staunchly against it. It didn't take me long to realize that it was yet another control tactic. He didn't want me to get a taste of life outside of the home, because that might make me remember what it felt like to be an independent woman.

That was unacceptable to him.

Still, I was clinging to the hope that I could get a job waitressing or something similar. I could probably learn quickly and hopefully, get cash tips. But so far, my can-do attitude had gotten me nowhere.

"I'm *borrrred*," Dominic complained from the backseat. I hadn't had a chance to meet anyone in town or find a babysitter yet, not that I loved the idea of him leaving my side, considering our situation. So, he was tagging along as I looked for a job, which might not be helping my chances of becoming employed.

Was I completely screwed here?

"How about we take an ice cream break?" I asked, deciding that I also needed a break from the disappointment of job hunting.

"Yes!" His shouted reply made me smile.

I remembered seeing a diner on the corner just down the street. Surely they'd have ice cream? After all, what kind of diner didn't have specialty shakes? Maybe I'd even get lucky, and they'd be hiring. A girl could dream.

The diner, named Tiny's, was busy for a weekday afternoon. Waitresses wearing shirts with the restaurant's logo on the front were bustling around the dining area, taking orders and bringing out trays full of food. I directed Dominic to one of the booths lining the wall, settling into the red vinyl seat.

"Welcome to Tiny's," a waitress with dark hair appeared beside us, placing two menus down on the table. "First-timers?"

"How did you know?" I asked.

"Just a hunch," she winked.

"Well, you're right," I confirmed. "We just moved to La Playa."

"Welcome," the waitress said, flashing a bright smile. "My name is Julie. What brings you to La Playa?"

"Uh..." I couldn't believe that I wasn't prepared for a question like this. "J-just needing a change. You know, I wanted to be closer to the ocean."

That sounded lame, but there was no way to take back the words now. Instead, I plowed ahead, "I'm Erica, and this is my son, Dominic. I was wondering, are you guys hiring?"

Julie shook her head, "Sorry, hun. But, you know what? I heard that the fitness studio was looking for someone to teach a class."

"What kind of class?" I had never done anything like that before, but maybe I could wing it.

"Yoga, I think." She shrugged.

Hope flared inside of my chest. I was *very* familiar with

yoga. I did it daily. In fact, my yoga mat was one of the few things that I made sure to bring with me when I fled my home.

"Where is this place?" I asked eagerly.

Julie pointed out that large front window of the diner. I followed her gaze, but frowned when I caught sight of the building across the street.

"Isn't that a bar?" The building had a neon sign hanging on the front, proclaiming it to be *The Blue Dog*, and the parking lot was full of motorcycles.

Julie chuckled. "Yes, but I was pointing down the block. The place is called Absolute Fitness."

I craned my neck and saw a white building with a glass front. It looked like a typical gym, but I hoped it could become so much more.

"Mom, are we going to have ice cream, or not?" Dominic interrupted our conversation, frowning.

"Oh, it's ice cream you're after? Well, we just so happen to have some of the best soft serve in town." Julie flipped over Dominic's menu for him, where there was a list of dessert options.

"Wow!"

His awe-filled voice was loud in the diner, and many people at nearby tables turned to look with amused expressions.

"Mom, can I have a banana split? Please?"

"Only if you eat something green with dinner."

"*Fine*," he mumbled.

"Two banana splits it is," I told Julie. After she walked away, I turned back to Dominic. "After our dessert, we're going to make one more stop."

"You want to go to that gym?"

"I want to work there. So, keep your fingers crossed for me, okay?"

"Okay," he agreed, literally crossing the middle and index fingers on both hands. I couldn't help but laugh. With that kind of support, I would get the job for sure.

THREE
TRAINER

I was a shitty cook. Always had been. It just wasn't my thing; I didn't have the patience for it. I generally sustained myself on fool-proof frozen meals that I could pop into the oven and food from Tiny's. I probably kept the damn place in business with how much money I spent there.

The only time I had good, homemade meals was on Sunday afternoons. Parking my bike on the driveway apron, I strode up to the brick-faced house that I had called home for a short period of time.

I never knew my dad. He walked out on my mom before I was even born. Some people might hate him for that, but after living with the unstable woman that gave birth to me, I couldn't exactly blame the guy for taking off. My mom never cared about anything more than Heroin. Some people might say that she had an illness and pity her. All I knew was that I was pretty much on my own for the first twelve years of my life, and it was impossible not to resent the woman that was supposed to give a damn about me. Instead, she neglected me until I was taken away by social services.

As far as I knew, she'd never even tried to change her ways and get me back.

Good riddance.

I was dumped into the foster care system, where I was shuffled around for four years. Some houses were better than others, but I'd been in a few terrible ones. I'd suffered abuse at the hands of men and women that were only foster parents because it came with a monthly check. The money was meant to be used to take care of me, but I'd generally been no better off than I was with my mother, who spent every dime she got her hands on buying her drugs.

Then, I was placed with Mama Tammy.

I didn't consider myself to be an overly sentimental man. With my childhood, I had to be tough to survive, so there wasn't room for that shit. But I loved Mama Tammy. She was the best foster parent I had, the only one that didn't give me back or make me so miserable that I ran away. I was with her for two years until I turned eighteen.

She didn't kick me out when I aged out of the system, but I knew that it was a financial strain once the money from the state stopped coming in. So, I set out on my own, getting an apartment in the complex owned by the Outlaw Souls. Most of us lived there, since we saw the club as more of a family than anything else. We were close, and we had each other's backs.

I made it a priority to return to visit her once a week, on Sunday afternoon. It wasn't always possible - life tended to get in the way sometimes - but I tried my damnedest to stop by.

This week, I was carrying a plastic bag from the hardware store at my side as I rang the doorbell. Mama Tammy pulled open the door seconds later, already wearing a bright smile.

"You're early," she said, pulling me into a hug. I could smell her floral perfume as I leaned down to wrap my arms around her plump body. She was several inches shorter than I was with dark brown skin and kinky, curly hair that she kept very short. I noticed that it was starting to turn grey, and I didn't like that. It reminded me that she was getting older.

"I figured I'd come a little early to have a look at the dryer before lunch," I explained. She'd told me two days ago that her dryer wasn't heating up, so I picked up a heating element this morning.

"You don't have to do that. I can hire a man," she said, but I could see the gratitude on her face.

"Or you can let me take care of it and save your money. After all, I owe you for all the food you give me every week."

"Oh, Raul, you can't fool me," she said, patting my cheek with the palm of her hand. She was the only person in my life that still called me by my given name. To everyone else, I was just "Trainer." I wouldn't know how to respond to anything else. "I think you just want to butter me up because you have a birthday coming up soon."

I smiled at her words. I had forgotten all about my birthday next month, but of course, she didn't. "You got me," I said, "Now how about I get to work while you finish lunch?"

"Okay, but don't work too hard. It's your day off."

I didn't bother telling her that I was basically self-employed and could take any day off I wanted. It felt good to know that she worried about me. It was something that had been missing from so much of my life that I clung to it now.

So, I made my way to the back of the house, pulling the dryer out from the wall and removing the back panel. I hunkered down and got to work, locating the heating element and disconnecting it before popping the new one into place. It was quick work, and twenty minutes later, I had put the thing back together and started it up.

Mama Tammy came into the laundry room, the open door allowing the enticing smell of fried chicken into the room. My stomach growled, reminding me that I had skipped breakfast. "Is it fixed?"

"I think so," I replied, opening the door and sticking my hand inside. I grinned and nodded, "We have heat," I confirmed.

"What would I do without you?" she reached out and ruffled my thick, black hair.

We made our way into the eat-in kitchen. The room was small and always seemed to be at least ten degrees hotter than the rest of the house, but it was cozy. Mama Tammy collected ceramic bears, and most of them were in this room, lining shelves and window sills. The curtains were white lace, and one end of the kitchen table always had a stack of unopened junk mail. I was sure that I looked completely out of place here in my leathers and riding boots. But Mama Tammy didn't care. She just sat a fully loaded plate on the table in front of me.

I wasted no time picking up a chicken leg and digging in. Flavor exploded in my mouth, making me groan.

"This is delicious," I told her, using my fork to scoop up some mashed potatoes.

"Don't talk with your mouth full," she said, but there was a small smile pulling at the corners of her mouth.

I took her advice and shut up while inhaling the food. She was also quiet, which was unusual. Normally, she filled our time together with chatter. Something must be on her mind.

Finally, when I finished off the last of the green beans on my plate, she spoke, "I need to tell you something."

I laid my fork down and gave her my full attention. "What is it?"

"It's not easy to tell you this...I know how you worry about me."

Unease made my stomach roll. "What is it?" I repeated.

"I've got a lump."

"What?" I furrowed my brow in confusion. "What are you talking about?"

"A lump on my breast. I have to go in for a biopsy next week."

I couldn't form words right away. I wasn't used to this kind of strong emotional distress, and it made my chest feel tight. Mama Tammy was the only person in my life outside of the Outlaw Souls, and the thought of losing her felt like drowning.

"I, uh, don't know what to say..." I swallowed. "Do they think it's..." I didn't want to say the C-word.

"They won't know until I get the results of the biopsy," she said, folding her hands on the table in front of her. "I was hoping you'd take me. I'll need a ride home afterward."

"Of course," I agreed quickly.

"It's on Monday morning."

"I'll pick you up."

"Not on that contraption outside," she added sternly. I surprised myself by breaking out into a full belly laugh, breaking the tension in the small room. She was always giving me a hard time about riding a bike and how unsafe she thought it was, and to hear her worrying about it now brought me back from the edge of panic. She was still the same old Mama Tammy that she'd always been, and no good would come from freaking out right now.

"Okay, okay. I'll bring the car. But I'm telling you, you'd love riding one. Feeling the air on your face... there's nothing like it."

"You're crazy," she shook her head.

"You know, I could even build you a custom chopper," I was teasing her, and she knew it. It was an old game of ours. I pretended that I could talk her into becoming a biker chick, and she sassed me back. It was exactly what I needed to forget about my worries. For now.

THE NEXT DAY was our monthly meeting of the Outlaw Souls. Sometimes we met more frequently, and we all spent a lot of time together, but Ryder liked for us to all get together at least once a month for an official meeting. They always took place in a backroom at The Blue Dog. Lately, we'd been working toward cleaning up La Playa, trying to take control of the town away from Las Balas, so that goal gave us plenty to discuss.

I was on my bike, taking the familiar route to the bar. The Blue Dog was located on the western side of La Playa, on the opposite street corner from Tiny's. There were several other businesses around, helping to make the bar seem less intimidating to those that weren't members of the club. That was important for us. It helped keep the cops off our backs.

I rode past a gas station and tire shop, weaving through the traffic on my Road King. Then, there was a second-hand clothing store on one side of the street, next to Absolute Fitness. Our Sergeant at Arms, Swole, was the manager of the gym, which was convenient for her, since it was located across the street and half a block down from The Blue Dog.

It was good for her to have a legitimate job like that. It gave her a little distance from Outlaw Souls on paper.

A red light at the corner made all traffic movements on the street stop just as I was in front of the gym. I put one foot down on the ground, to keep my balance, and waited. Movement out of the corner of my eye drew my attention to a woman that was leaving Absolute Fitness with a black gym bag hanging off of one shoulder. She was average height and curvy, with her skinny jeans hugging her ass in a way that made my eye wander without my conscious consent. The shirt she was wearing had a V-neck that showed just a hint of cleavage.

Damn. She had a body that was built for sin.

My eyes greedily drank her in. Her dark hair was damp, as if she'd just finished showering, and that thought caused a mental image to appear that had my body coming to life. Suddenly, this mystery woman turned to look my way, as if she felt my eyes running over her. Bright green orbs stared at me, surrounded by dark eyelashes. She had high cheekbones and a button nose, but it was her mouth that drew my attention, with its perfect cupid's bow lips. I'd never felt such an instant attraction to a woman before. Every part of my body hardened just from looking at her.

She was watching me too, seemingly unable to tear her eyes away from my heated stare. The woman was still walking down the sidewalk, but I had distracted her. Her foot caught on a raised section of the sidewalk, making her stumble forward. It happened so quickly, and before I could even react, she had gone down on the concrete, barely throwing her hand out in time.

"Shit," I muttered. Bringing my bike over to the curb, I brought down the kickstand and hopped off, hurrying to her. She was already getting back to her feet by the time I reached her, looking down at her scraped palm with a frown and reddening cheeks. "Are you okay?" I asked, stopping beside her. I reached out to place a hand on her back, but she flinched, so I pulled my hand back.

"Uh... yeah," she said, shrugging as if it was no big deal.

"Are you hurt?"

"Well, my pride is a little bruised, but other than that, I'll be fine." She gave me a weak smile, a blush still coloring her cheeks. I smirked. It looked like my girl was a tough one.

Wait a minute. *My girl?* Where did that thought come from? I didn't even know this woman's name.

"What about your hand?" I asked even as she fisted it and brought it to her side, clearly trying to hide the wound from my view.

"I've had worse."

I didn't like that at all. Her matter-of-fact tone made it seem like her words didn't matter, but they sure as hell did to me. I wasn't even sure why.

"I'm Trainer," I said, sticking out my hand for her to shake. It occurred to me that some women might be intimidated by a biker guy approaching them on the street, especially one that looked like me. I was big. Not just muscular, but broad and tall. But this woman didn't look scared.

In fact, now that I was closer to her, I could see that she was a fighter. I wasn't sure exactly how I could tell, maybe it was something in her eyes or the way she held herself, but I had the distinct impression that I was looking at a warrior right now.

"Erica," she said, taking my hand with her uninjured one and giving it a surprisingly firm shake.

"Hey, Trainer." I turned and saw that Swole had just walked out of the gym, shrugging on her jacket with the patch sewed into the back. "You coming to the meeting?"

Swole's eyes went back and forth between me and Erica, lingering on our hands, which were still clasped together. I quickly let go, immediately missing her warmth.

What was going on with me? I felt almost frazzled around this woman, which was so out of character for me.

"Yeah. Sure," I replied. "See ya around," I nodded to Erica, who was still looking at me like I was somehow fascinating.

"Right. Nice to meet you," she said. Then, turning to Swole, "and I'll see you tomorrow."

Swole walked to the curb, waiting for the traffic to thin out so she could cross, while I mounted my bike once again, driving it across the street to the bar. I was damn close to being late for the meeting, but for once, I didn't care. My mind was too preoccupied with a brunette. I couldn't resist looking back across the street once I'd parked in The Blue Dog's parking lot, but she was already gone.

FOUR

ERICA

Don't even think about it.

I had to repeat this to myself three times as I watched Trainer throw a thick leg over his motorcycle and ride it to the bar across the street. I couldn't let myself get involved with a man right now. Maybe not ever again.

Hadn't I learned my lesson? Men were trouble.

And this man? The leather-bound, mountain of a man that looked just a little *too* wild with his curly black hair and full, matching beard? There was no way hooking up with him would be a good idea.

Yet, I didn't get any feelings of menace from him. I could barely register anything other than the desire flooding my body. I hadn't felt this attracted to a man in years, if ever. Maybe it was that wild quality that I knew should keep me away. Maybe it was the muscles that I could tell he had, even under his leather jacket. Maybe it was the concern in his eyes when he hopped off the bike to make sure I was okay.

It didn't matter. I needed to focus on building a life for

my son and keeping both of us safe. I didn't need a sexy distraction.

Besides, it probably wasn't a mutual attraction. Mortification slammed into me as I recalled my tumble onto the sidewalk. I'd gotten too distracted ogling Trainer, and humiliated myself. He must have thought I was such an idiot...

With that thought in mind, I turned away from The Blue Dog and made my way down the sidewalk. Getting into my car, I checked the time on my cheap burner phone. I had ten minutes before I had to pick Dominic up from the babysitter.

I hated being away from him, especially now that we were in hiding from Jeff, but after I'd met with Swole on Friday, I had known that I had no choice. To my delight, I got the job teaching yoga classes at the fitness studio.

When I showed up asking about an application that afternoon, Swole had been standing at the front counter. She had introduced herself to me as Susie Holt, and I almost laughed. She did *not* look like a Susie. When she asked that I call her by her nickname, Swole, I quickly agreed. Somehow, that name suited her much better.

Swole invited me into her office for an interview on the spot, even with Dominic tagging along. Of course, a seven-year-old boy wasn't going to sit by quietly while adults talked, especially not after consuming all the sugar in a banana split. I was nervous about his presence tanking the interview, but Swole shocked me by pulling a box of legos out of the bottom drawer of her desk and inviting Dominic to scoot his chair closer to the edge of her desk and play with them. When I sent her a questioning look, she showed me a picture on her desk of herself with another woman and little boy that couldn't be older than five. Apparently, her wife worked at the fitness center too, and their son often spent time there after school.

Just like that, I relaxed. Swole might be the most muscular woman I'd ever seen - hell, she was built bigger than most men I knew - and I sensed that she was *not* a woman to be trifled with, but hearing the affection in her voice when she spoke about her son made me feel like we had some common ground.

Still, I knew it was a long shot when we started talking about the position. I had to admit that I had never taught yoga before, but I was quick to assure her that I was no novice. I had been doing yoga for years, ever since I had started to help get back into shape when Dominic was born.

Swole seemed completely on board, despite my inexperience, until I confessed that I needed to be paid in cash, with no paper trail. She had paused and stared at me for a long time through narrowed eyes. I felt like I was under a microscope and had to force myself not to squirm. She must have seen something revealing in my expression, because hers softened, and she told me that we could work something out.

I could hardly believe my luck and spent the whole weekend researching tips and techniques for teaching yoga. The toughest thing was finding a babysitter for Dominic. Jeff had kept us isolated as well as he could for so long that I wasn't used to being away from my son for any length of time. Add in the looming threat of Jeff somehow hunting us down, and I was a nervous wreck about dropping him off with a sitter.

But I understood that this was a part of life as a single mother.

So, I turned to social media. Finding a mom group in the area, I asked for recommendations. That was how I found a former elementary school teacher named Jennifer that had an in-home daycare. The other three children she babysat were around Dominic's age, and all of their mothers sang her praises. I just hoped that Dominic made friends with the others. He needed a few friends. We both did.

Starting the car, I merged into traffic. The babysitter's house was on the opposite side of La Playa, but it was worth the drive to know that Dominic was in good hands. I gripped the steering wheel, and a stinging sensation in my left hand reminded me that I had a scrape to tend to when we got home. I hadn't been lying to Trainer when I said that I'd had worse. There were still bruises on my ribs that ached worse than this flesh wound. Jeff's obsession with appearances meant that he was always careful when he took his anger out on me. The last thing he wanted was for anyone to see the bruises. It would tarnish his reputation. My face was off-limits. Usually my arms too. But parts of my body that were always covered by clothes were free game.

Bastard.

I tried to force those thoughts to the back of my mind as I neared the babysitter's house. I needed to wear my poker face for Dominic.

When I rang the doorbell of Jennifer's house, the thundering sound of running feet could be heard on the other side of the door.

"Don't answer the door, guys. Only adults can do that." Jennifer's patient voice could be heard clearly.

"But it's my dad," a young girl's voice replied.

"Huh-uh," a boy replied. "It's *my* mom."

I didn't hear Dominic's voice, but I hoped that he was there with the other kids.

"Why don't you let me open it, and we'll see?" Jennifer suggested.

When she pulled open the door, I was met with four eager faces staring up at me, practically buzzing with excitement.

"Ha!" Dominic cried out triumphantly. "It's mine."

The kids all jostled each other playfully, and I felt a stinging at the back of my eyes. I had never seen him like this. So carefree and playful. It was like he always repressed a part of himself before now, and he was starting to open himself up and be a kid for the first time. We had been in La Playa less than a week, and the kid was blossoming.

"How was he?" I asked Jennifer, glad that my voice didn't betray how choked up I felt. I stepped inside, closing the door behind myself. The kids were thoroughly distracted by their chattering, not paying any attention to the two of us.

"A little shy at first," Jennifer said, watching the kids as we talked. "But, as you can see, he started coming out of his shell after a while."

I could see that. I just hoped that he remembered our story. Even telling other children the truth about us could put us in danger.

We left Jennifer's house shortly after that, driving to our new home. I passed three motorcycles on the way, making me think of Trainer. I'd never been on a bike before, and the idea of being on the back of his Harley, with our bodies pressed tightly together, made a warm pool in my belly.

So much for not thinking about it.

"So, how did you like Jennifer's?" I asked Dominic, who had been quietly sitting in his booster seat, playing with an old Gameboy that had been mine when I was a child. I'd come across it when I was preparing to leave Jeff and gave it to Dominic to give him something to do on the long drive here.

"It was fun," he said. I glanced in the rearview mirror and saw that he wasn't even looking up from the game system in his hand. Well, I guessed that I couldn't exactly expect to compete with the game for his full attention.

"And you liked the other kids? What did you guys talk about?"

Now he paused the game and looked up at me, probably hearing the concern in my voice. "I remembered everything you told me," he assured me, sounding so much like an adult that I immediately wanted to end the conversation. But I couldn't.

"Our name? Where we're from? Who your dad is?"

"Yeah. I *told* you."

"Okay, I believe you."

I had no choice. I couldn't be with him twenty-four hours a day.

When we pulled up in front of the duplex, I got my first glimpse of my neighbor. In the days that we had been living here, I had heard the neighbors plenty, mostly shouting matches between a man and woman or a child screaming in the way that toddlers do when throwing a fit, but I hadn't actually caught sight of a person.

The woman was sitting in a lawn chair on her half of the front porch, smoking a cigarette. Her hair was in a messy bun, and she was wearing bright pink pajama pants and a large hooded sweatshirt. She eyed us curiously as I helped Dominic out of the car. It came as no surprise when she spoke to me as we climbed the porch steps.

"What's your name?" she asked.

"Go on inside," I told Dominic, handing him the house key. I didn't want to be stuck up, but I didn't like the look of this woman. She had an almost predatory look in her eye that I didn't trust. I would do the neighborly thing and talk to her, but I didn't want Dominic to be a part of it. "I'm Erica. Erica Mills."

I was holding my gym bag in one hand and my burner phone in the other, which were good excuses not to offer to shake her hand without seeming rude.

"Erica, huh?" she said, taking a long drag off her cigarette. "You don't look like an Erica."

I wasn't sure how to respond to that, but it made a sliver of unease trail down my spine because it wasn't my real name.

"I'm Talia," she said, rising from her chair. As she moved closer to me, so that only the half-wall dividing the porch separated us, a cloud of smoke drifted toward me, and I couldn't suppress a cough. "Was that your little boy?"

"Yeah." *Of course, it was.* "That's Dominic."

"I've seen you guys coming and going. No man, though. His dad a deadbeat?"

I was surprised to hear that she'd seen us. Was she watching us through her windows?

"I'm a widow," I said, following the story I'd made up and not elaborating.

"Damn, girl. That sucks. Even though I sometimes wish my old man would bite the big one," she laughed like she'd told me a hilarious joke. My dislike grew.

I studied Talia. She might be around my age of twenty-seven, but it was hard to tell. She was rough around the edges, with dark circles under her eyes and dull, brown eyes. She was thin, almost too thin, and her skin seemed loose, the way it would if she lost weight very quickly. I knew it was shitty to make assumptions, but I couldn't help thinking that she looked like she used some kind of heavy drugs. She was definitely not a healthy person.

"You live here with your husband?" I asked, wondering

if that was the person I'd heard her arguing with nearly every evening.

"Nah," she shook her head and dropped her cigarette butt onto her side of the porch, where it joined at least a dozen others. "We ain't married, but he's my kid's dad. So, I guess I'm stuck with him."

She didn't actually sound sad about that. It was more like she was telling a joke. She clearly had no idea what it was like to really be stuck with a man. It wasn't amusing in the least.

But I knew that she had no knowledge of my personal situation.

"What's your story?" Talia asked. "Why did you come to La Playa?"

I was spared having to answer as we were both distracted by the roar of a motorcycle's engine as it rounded the corner. *How many people around here are bikers?*

Talia stepped away from me, a smile stretching across her face. The man on the bike came up onto the sidewalk, parking it on the walkway leading to their side of the porch. When he dismounted, his back was to me for a brief moment, and I saw that the patch on the back of his jacket was different than the one I had spotted on Swole and Trainer's jackets. This one had a skull with a bullet between its teeth and the words La Balas. It looked... sinister. I wasn't sure what else I expected from a motorcycle club emblem, but for some reason, the sight of it made a shiver go down my spine.

I stood there awkwardly, watching as Talia met the man at the porch steps, jumping into his arms and wrapping her legs around his waist. They kissed, and I decided it was a good time to take my leave. I was no prude, and was harboring some dirty thoughts about a hunky biker myself, but watching my neighbors share this intimate moment was not my idea of a good time. And leaving gave me an easy out of the conversation.

I went into the house and started cooking dinner for Dominic, determining that it would be best to avoid the neighbors as much as possible. I wasn't sure how easy that would be in a shared duplex, but I was going to try. Something in my gut told me that they were the kind of trouble I didn't need.

FIVE
TRAINER

Rock music was blaring in the garage as I put the Triumph up on the center stand. It was a new purchase and didn't require a ton of work, but I still thought that I could fix it up a bit and sell it for a profit. First things first, the thing was overdue for an oil change. Removing the drain plug, I let the old oil leak out into the drain pan while I sipped on my bottle of beer. It always took a while to make sure all the old shit was completely out, but I didn't mind. It was worth taking my time and doing it right.

Once the oil had finished draining, I replaced the filter with a new one, and added fresh oil. Letting the bike run for a few minutes so that the oil could work through the system, I washed my hands in the old utility sink in the corner of the garage.

Ortega's Auto used to be owned by our old president, Padre, but since his death, ownership had transferred to his brother. Since he had enough on his plate with The Blue Dog, Padre had allowed Ryder to pretty much take over running the auto shop. It worked out well that way since Ryder had been working at the shop for years.

I wasn't an employee of Ortega's Auto, but Ryder let me use the shop to fix up my bikes, as long as I bought my own parts and tools. I didn't have a garage at the apartment complex, so it was a lifesaver.

"A Bonneville?" A voice behind me spoke, barely audible over the music.

Turning away from the sink, I grabbed a roll of paper towels to dry my hands. Swole was standing next to the bike, looking it over. Of all the people in the Outlaw Souls, she and I had the greatest appreciation for European bikes. Everyone was crazy about riding, of course, and every member spent time wrenching on their own Harleys; but I found the Ducatis, BMWs, and Triumphs just as interesting.

"Yep," I said nodding. I stepped over to the old stereo on the workbench and turned down the music. "You're looking at a '79 T140."

"Nice," Swole ran a hand down the white gas tank, admiring the machine. "That was back when they still had kickstarters, right?"

I nodded. "She's a 750cc parallel-twin," I gave her the basic stats.

After we'd both taken our time examining the bike, she got to the point of tracking me down here. "I'm here on club business."

"What is it?" I asked, crossing my arms over my chest. When Swole got serious, it was important to pay attention.

"That ride you're planning, the big one. It can't happen."

The big one was a ride to the Grand Staircase-Escalante National Monument in Utah. It would be the biggest ride the club had taken since before I was a member, spanning a couple of days, but it should be worth it. The beauty of the area was supposed to be something special to behold, and the twisty roads that cut paths through the region seemed as if they were made for adventure riding.

"Why not?" I couldn't hide the disappointment in my voice, but I wasn't going to argue with her. When the Sergeant at Arms made a proclamation like that, she usually had a good reason.

"This." She pulled a small baggie out of her jacket pocket and held it up for me to see. The crystalline white powder was unmistakable.

"Meth." I shook my head in disgust. That shit was poison. "Where'd you get that?"

"I've got a connection through the fitness club that keeps an eye on drug dealings in the area since Outlaw Souls started cleaning this shit up. She brought it to me. I'll give you three guesses what the source is."

I only needed one. "Las Balas."

"You got it. I've already talked to Ryder, and we'll go over it at the next meeting, but I wanted to let you know that the Utah ride was going to have to be postponed. We need all hands on deck to track down the source of this shit and get it out of our city."

"Fuck," I grumbled, shaking my head. I understood where she was coming from, priorities and all that, but that didn't mean I was happy about it. "Alright, we'll postpone. But I'm still taking us. It'll be a great ride, worth the wait."

"Deal," she agreed, bumping knuckles with me.

I decided it was a good time to take a break, so I walked out of the shop at Swole's side, locking up behind myself since the other guys were still at lunch. The day was a cloudy one, threatening rain.

"So... are you going to ask about her?"

I didn't have to question who Swole was talking about.

Erica hadn't been far from my mind since I met her two days ago. I found her at the forefront of my thoughts way too often, considering that I barely knew the woman. Even more troubling was the way that my body reacted just at the thought of her. My blood was roaring.

"Are you going to tell me about her?" I responded, earning a rare smile from her.

"Maybe a little. She's secretive, so I don't know much."

"Single?"

"I think so. But she's got a kid."

"Really?" I wasn't sure what to think about that. I'd never dated a woman with a kid before, assuming that they were too complicated. A woman's baggage didn't get much heavier than that.

"Little boy. He seems like a good kid, but he's young, so keep that in mind if you run into her again."

I was sure that I would. In fact, I was tempted to go join the damn fitness center just to orchestrate such a thing. But did I want to go after her knowing that she was a mom? My cock, heavy in my pants at the thought of her curvy body, wanted to scream "yes," but I wasn't so sure. She was hot, but I didn't know anything about kids. What if she expected me to play the part of dad? I didn't think I had it in me.

SOME BARS THRIVED ONLY on the weekends, but The Blue Dog wasn't like that. It seemed that there was always a crowd here, even on a Wednesday night. I never sat at the tables that were scattered around the place, preferring to perch myself on a barstool.

"Another one?" Carlos asked, nodding to the empty beer bottle in front of me. I nodded.

Carlos had started working at The Blue Dog five years ago, and became a Prospect almost immediately, sponsored by Hawk. He'd finally been voted in as a member and received his patch last year.

Carlos sat another bottle on the bar in front of me, twisting the top off. I let my eyes roam the bar as I took a swig and let out a contented sigh. The first sip was always the best.

There were several Outlaw Souls in the bar, but also others from the community. Some I recognized, some I didn't. You didn't have to be a member of the motorcycle club to enjoy this place, but here were always patrons that stuck out, ones that didn't quite belong. I watched a group of women that fit that bill crowded around a table, knocking back tequila shots and giggling way too much.

That was common here, young women that came in to satisfy their curiosity about the club members. Usually, they stayed in groups, flirted with anyone in a leather jacket, and left with a story about how daring and wild they were for visiting a known biker bar. Sometimes, they were legitimately looking for a hookup. Those women were bold and, in my experience, great for a round or two in bed, but the thrill wore off quickly for them. This lifestyle wasn't for everyone, and it would be delusional to make more out of a bar hook-up than there was.

I saw Pin at the pool tables, getting his ass kicked by the girl that he'd been seeing for a year. A pang of loneliness echoed in the center of my chest. Not long ago, I was content with the single life. There were always women around to fulfill my sexual needs, and I had never had a more meaningful relationship, so I didn't give much thought to what I might be missing. Then, Ryder fell for a girl that made him a better man. Not long after, Pin met Claire.

I could see a change in both men since they found their significant others. They hadn't necessarily been unhappy before, but now they were... *fulfilled*. They had something that I never knew I wanted.

The evening sunlight spilled over me as the door of the bar opened. The two girls that walked in, definitely belonged in the "don't quite belong" category. They were young, with manicures and mile-high heels. Heavy makeup coated both of their faces, which I suspected was an attempt to make them look older than they were.

The girls approached the bar, where Carlos was already watching them with pursed lips and narrowed eyes. "IDs, ladies," he demanded, holding out his hand.

They didn't hesitate. Reaching into tiny handbags, they each produced a driver's license and handed it over. Carlos looked them over for a moment, unsure.

"Let me see," a voice said to my right. I glanced over and saw that Hawk had appeared at some point, taking a seat beside me.

Carlos gave Hawk the IDs, looking relieved. Hawk earned a hell of a lot of cash in the fake ID business himself, and it was common knowledge that he could make the best papers in La Playa. A smile stretched across his face as he looked at the girl's IDs.

"Good ones, I'll give you that," he said, looking at the pouting minors. "But not good enough. They're fakes."

"No, they're not," one of the girls replied, glaring.

"Should we call the cops to be sure?" Hawk asked. The girls couldn't know that he was bluffing. We'd never willingly call the cops here.

"We'll leave," the other girl hastily cut in, reaching for the IDs. Hawk pulled away, tucking the IDs into his pocket.

"I'll hold onto these. To teach you a lesson."

The first girl looked like she wanted to argue, but her friend placed a hand on her arm and shook her head.

"Asshole," she muttered under her breath as her friend practically dragged her out the door.

"She has a point," I said once the girls were outside. "Kind of an asshole move to take the IDs."

Hawk shrugged. "The last thing we need is to get popped for serving minors. The next ones might think twice about pulling this shit in here if word gets around that they lose their fake IDs."

I grinned. "Genius."

"Asshole genius," Hawk clinked his beer bottle against mine. "I'll take it."

We both drank to that.

SIX
ERICA

It was Friday afternoon, and I'd just completed my final yoga class of the day. As everyone cleared out of the room, I stayed behind to tidy up. Rolling up my yoga mat, I tucked it into my duffle bag before pulling out my water bottle and taking several big gulps.

I had done it. I had made it through my first week of yoga classes, and I was pretty sure that it went well. At least, I hadn't gotten any complaints. A heady feeling of accomplishment had me grinning like a crazy person as I walked out of the room.

"What's put that look on your face?" Tammie, Swole's wife, asked as she caught sight of me. She was a pilates instructor, and we had become friends in the past week.

"Just happy about this job," I said honestly. I had met Jeff when I was eighteen years old and married him a year later. I didn't have experience in the working world, and it surprised me how much I enjoyed knowing that I was earning my own money doing something that I enjoyed. I had never had that before.

"Oh, to be young and hopeful like that again," Tammie

replied wistfully. I laughed as we started walking toward the locker rooms.

"What are you talking about?" I asked, looking her over. "You can't be any older than thirty-five."

"Thirty-eight," she corrected, "but thanks for that."

"Anyway, I like this job. Are you saying that you don't enjoy teaching pilates?"

"Sure," she shrugged. "But the excitement has faded slightly after six years. I'm glad that you're happy here, though. The last yoga teacher was a real bitch."

That was what I liked about Tammy. She was always straight with you, saying what she really thought. After years of mind games from Jeff, I found that I appreciated directness above anything else.

We stepped into separate shower pods, and I quickly went through the process of washing my hair and body. By the time Tammie was done, I was already dressed in jeans and a t-shirt, braiding my hair in one plait.

"What are your plans for the evening?" she asked as she dried her pixie-cut blonde hair.

"I'm picking Dominic up from daycare at five."

She waited a moment for me to continue. When I didn't, she frowned, "And then?"

"And then, nothing. I'll make dinner and maybe read a book or something when he's asleep."

"Oh my God, I almost died of boredom just listening to that. It's *Friday night*."

"I know that." My voice sounded defensive, even to my ears. "I'm a mom. I can't just go out and party every weekend."

"I'm a mom, too."

"I'm a *single* mom."

"All the more reason to go out. It's tough being a single

parent. You need a break every now and then."

"I love Dominic." There was that defensiveness again. The truth was, I did like the idea of an evening off, a chance to go out and enjoy myself for the first time in years. But didn't that make me a bad mother?

"We all love our kids. That doesn't mean that we stop existing as individuals once they're born. You are a twenty-something single woman in a new town. You can't tell me you have no interest in exploring the nightlife."

I nibbled on my bottom lip. "My babysitter only does her in-home daycare during the day. And you're right I'm new in town. I don't know anyone that I trust to watch him last minute like this."

"Swole and I are going out for a couple of drinks tonight. Will you join us if my niece, Heather, will watch Dominic along with my son? She's a great girl. I trust her completely"

"I don't know…"

It *did* make sense. If Tammy trusted Heather to babysit her son, Emory, then surely Dominic would be okay for a couple hours, right? I wasn't sure why I was so reluctant.

Tammy placed a hand on my shoulder and leveled me with a serious stare. "You are not irresponsible if you go out tonight."

I felt myself relax at her words. I could tell she was sincere, and somehow she hit the nail on the head. I was feeling like a reckless, irresponsible mom, but that wasn't fair. Dominic was my entire world. I would do anything for him. All that didn't get erased just because I wanted to have a girls night. I'd never gone to a bar with friends before. Jeff and I had married before I was even old enough to legally drink. By the time I turned twenty-one, he was completely running my life. I didn't have any friends.

"Okay," I nodded, "but only if Heather is okay with watching him too."

Tammy called Heather to confirm, while I packed away my shower things. Nerves and anticipation battling for dominance in the pit of my stomach. I couldn't wait to see how this aspect of my life turned out.

"CAN I bring my walking dinosaur toy? And my nerf guns? And my Gameboy?"

Dominic was practically bouncing with excitement as he loaded up his backpack with as many toys as he could fit. He was eager to meet a new friend, even if he was a couple of years younger than Dominic. I was starting to realize just how important interaction was for a child and how much of that Dominic had missed out on.

"Not the Gameboy. That's really a one-person gaming system, and I don't want you guys fighting over it."

"Okay," he complied easily, taking the Gameboy out of the bag. The thing was so old, and I only had one Mario game for it, that I thought, I should look into getting him a more recent gaming system. Maybe one with two players. I hadn't done it in the past because I didn't want him to spend all his time staring at a television screen, but he was getting older now, and I thought he could handle it now.

I left him in his bedroom, stuffing that backpack, and went into my room. It was sparsely furnished, with just a queen bed and a chest of drawers that I'd gotten cheap at a second-hand store because it was pretty badly scuffed up. Going to my closet, I looked through the clothing there, trying to find something that would be fitting to wear to a bar, since Tammy had told me that we were going to The

Blue Dog. Apparently, all the bikers that were in the Outlaw Souls motorcycle club hung out there. That explained why I'd seen Swole and Trainer going over there just days ago.

Flicking through the hangers of clothing, I finally stopped when I came to dress that I'd never worn. It still had the tags on it, even though it was bought two years ago. I wasn't sure why I even purchased the thing. It was a black dress that was short and hugged my curves. Jeff would never have let me go out in public dressed in that. He'd tell me that it would make him look bad if I dressed like a whore and that no one was allowed to see me except him.

Fuck. Him.

Grabbing the dress, and I pulled it out, looking it over. No frills or accents, just soft black fabric. I closed my bedroom door before stripping down and pulling it over my head. The hem of the dress came down to my mid-thigh, exposing much more leg than I was used to. I looked myself over in my full-length mirror with a critical eye, but then Dominic pushed open the bedroom door and walked in.

"Wow, mom, you look pretty."

His blunt honestly melted my heart. "You think so?"

"Yeah, but I like your red hair more."

So did I, but the dark brown was growing on me. I would have to keep the roots touched up so that no one knew it was dyed at all.

Tousling my hair so that it fell in waves around my head, I put on minimal makeup and slipped into some low-heeled shoes. No need to break my neck with a towering heel.

Grabbing my purse, I glanced inside at the envelope that held the cash I'd brought with me when I left Jeff. It was thinner than I would have thought possible after such a short period of time, but at least I had a job. I wouldn't get my first paycheck until next week, so this cash had to last until then.

"Let's go, Bud," I called out to Dominic. He came hurrying into the room, his backpack full to bursting. "You know you're only going to be there for a couple of hours, right?"

"Mom, you don't understand."

Well, he had me there.

Leaving the house, I paused to lock the front door. When I turned back around, Talia's - *boyfriend? baby-daddy?* - whatever he was, he was walking up the steps on their half of the porch. He stared straight at my breasts, and I suppressed a shiver of disgust at the unmistakable lust in his expression. This guy was such a creep.

Looking away, I acted like he wasn't there at all. Dominic was waiting for me at the car, so we climbed in and took off for the babysitter's place. I didn't look back at the duplex, but the hairs standing up on the back of my neck told me that he was watching me until we finally turned a corner and were out of sight.

When I dropped Dominic off at Heather's home, which was a ground-floor apartment, he jumped right into playing with Swole's little boy, just giving me a quick goodbye hug. He was growing up so fast.

I traveled the now familiar path toward work, but instead of parking in the lot of the fitness center, I continued further down the street and turned into The Blue Dog's parking lot. It was packed. Motorcycles took up the spaces closest to the building, and there must have been twenty, maybe thirty of them. A sea of shiny chrome exhausts and black leather seats being watched over by a thin man with a bandana tied around his head. Much of the rest of the spaces in the lot were taken up by cars, and I added my own to their number.

I could hear loud music playing as I got closer to the building, and when I pulled the door open, my senses were overwhelmed by the mass of people and the volume of their conversations combined with the music. I slipped inside, scanned the crowd for Tammy or Swole. Finally, I caught sight of my muscular boss and relaxed. She was sitting at a square table halfway across the room, throwing back a shot of something amber-colored.

As I started to make my way to her, my eye drifted toward the bar, clashing with Trainer's burning gaze. I watched as he deliberately looked over every inch of my body, his stare so intense that it almost felt like a physical caress. Every part of my body seemed to tingle, as his eyes passed over it, I was so aware of him.

This didn't feel like the unwanted leering of my neighbor. No, this was raw and mutual. Trainer's jacket was thrown over the back of his stool, and the black t-shirt he wore stretched over his wide chest, doing nothing to conceal the hard muscles beneath. I could see that he had a full sleeve tattoo on his left arm and had the urge to examine it closer, running my fingers over the ink. Although, if I were close enough to touch him, I couldn't see myself stopping at his arm…

Stop it. The little voice in my head that knew dating this man was a bad idea spoke up. I blinked and tore my eyes away from him. I wasn't here to meet *him*.

Yet, once I joined Swole and Tammy at their table, I couldn't seem to stop myself from looking over at Trainer every few minutes. Why did he have to be so hot?

"You know, we can invite him to join us," Tammy said, bringing my full attention back to her.

"Who?" I asked, though I knew damn well who she was talking about.

"Trainer. He's a friend, an Outlaw Soul."

"What exactly does it mean to be an Outlaw Soul?" I asked. I could guess that they were some kind of group of bikers, but I didn't know anything about that.

"I'm not one," Tammy said. "but Swole is. They're a motorcycle club. A group of people that enjoy riding."

"That's it?" I asked incredulously.

"Well, it *is* a club," Swole explained. "You have to earn your place here, and we have goals and rules. But we're a family."

I had a feeling there might be more to it, perhaps some shady or illegal activities, but maybe I was letting my imagination go wild based on the way TV shows and movies portrayed these clubs.

"So, do you want us to invite him over?" Tammy pressed.

"Oh... uh, no. You don't need to do that."

"Really? Because you guys have been eye-fucking since the moment you walked in the door."

"No, we haven't." I denied weakly, but I couldn't seem to keep myself from looking over at him once again. What I saw made my blood boil. A stick-thin blonde wearing a dress that left absolutely nothing to the imagination had approached him. If she were standing any closer to him, she'd be sitting in his lap.

Trainer's face was blocked by her big, curly hair, so I couldn't tell if he was interested in her or not, but that didn't stop the jealousy from taking root. Suddenly, staying away from him became a whole lot harder. I might barely know him, but that didn't seem to matter.

I wanted him to be mine.

SEVEN

TRAINER

"How about we get out of here?"

I stared at the woman, practically draping herself all over me, trying to recall her name. I hadn't been paying attention when she first approached and introduced herself. Was it Amy? Ally?

Who cares.

I wasn't interested. Well, not interested in *her*. My mind and body were both too occupied with Erica.

"No thanks, I want to stay here," I said. No point in beating around the bush. She could move along to someone else. I saw Moves shoot me a surprised look from the other side of the blonde woman, like he couldn't believe I would pass up a sure thing.

"Well, we can do it here," she suggested, practically purring as she ran her french-tipped fingers along my arm. "This place must have a bathroom. Or maybe the alley outside, if you want a little public action."

I shook my head, trying not to chuckle. "Look, Abby, I-"

"It's Ashley," she interrupted, sticking out her lower lip

in a pout that wasn't nearly as cute as she probably thought it was.

"Ashley, you're barking up the wrong tree. I suggest you look elsewhere for your good time." The rumble in my voice made it clear that it wasn't really a suggestion.

"Your loss," she said coolly, stepping away. I watched as she zeroed in on another target, Ryder, and couldn't suppress my laugh this time. Tonight just wasn't her night.

"Are you crazy?" Moves asked.

"Just not interested."

"Young, hot, and no strings attached. What is she offering that you *don't* want?"

"Maybe I want the strings," I replied, glancing over at Erica once again.

She was already looking my way with a frown on her face. The fire in her eyes wasn't desire this time. She looked pissed.

Why was that so hot?

Picking up my half-empty beer, I stood.

"Where are you going?" Moves asked.

"I'm gonna go get what I *do* want." Erica's eyes widened as I approached her table, stopping at the empty seat between her and Swole. "Can I sit here?"

"Sure," Erica said, her voice taking on a husky quality as she spoke.

I settled into the seat, looking at the three women around me. "Hope I'm not intruding on a girls night out."

"Not at all," Tammy quickly assured me. Her smile and the way her eyes flitted back and forth between me and Erica made it clear that she saw the chemistry between us. I was sure that everyone did. It felt too powerful to ignore.

Swole didn't say anything, but rolled her eyes at me. For

someone that had been married to the love of her life for damn near twelve years, she was hopelessly unromantic.

"Actually, Tammy and I were just about to play a game at one of the tables," Swole said, nodding to the pool tables on the far side of the room.

"We were?" Tammy asked. Swole gave her an impatient look. "Right. We were."

They both stood and scampered away.

"Well, good thing that wasn't completely obvious, huh?" Erica asked, flashing me a small grin that brought a dimple in her cheek.

Yeah, they were obvious about it, but I was glad to have this time alone with Erica. Well, as alone as I could get while in a crowded bar.

"They mean well," I told her.

"I'm sure. They're the whole reason I'm here tonight. Tammy talked me into it."

"I'm glad." Reaching out, I laid my hand on top of her smaller one on the table. "I'd been hoping to run into you again, but I'm not exactly the yoga type."

"You sure? Lot's of men do it."

"Men like me?" I asked, raising an eyebrow.

"Well... no," she admitted. "You do seem more like a weightlifter."

I flexed my arm muscles, and she giggled, slapping my chest playfully. Erica's phone buzzed on the table, and she picked it up. I saw that it was a text message notification, but looked away so that I wasn't reading it over her shoulder. She took a moment to type a quick reply before setting the phone down and turning back to me.

"Sorry about that. I left my son with a new babysitter, and I asked her to check in with me occasionally."

Erica paused, watching me closely, an almost defiant

look in her eye. I had the feeling she was looking for my reaction to the news of her kid. It felt like a test. Normally, I didn't go in for mind games like that, but I couldn't help admiring her for putting her kid first. I had no doubt that if I showed displeasure about there being a kid in the picture that she would end this before it even started.

"What's his name?"

Surprise flickered across her face, but she recovered quickly. "Dominic. This is him."

Opening her phone, she showed me the background picture. It was a picture of Erica with her arms wrapped around a young boy as they both smiled at the camera. They both looked happy, and Erica's hair was different.

"So, you used to be a redhead?"

"What?" Erica went pale, as she turned, and saw the picture she'd shown me. "No, no. That's not. I mean, obviously I did have red hair, but I didn't mean for you to see that."

She fumbled with the phone in her hand, trying to lock it. I saw that her hands were shaking. *What the hell?*

Reaching out, I placed both of my hands over her own, stilling them. Erica looked up into my eyes, and I was sure that I saw fear there. Something strange was going on here, and she was clearly rattled. I didn't understand what had triggered it, but I wanted to somehow soothe her.

"Then I didn't see it," I said. "Forget it even happened."

"Are you sure?" she asked. "I know it's weird, but I just... I didn't like my hair like that."

She was a bad liar. Not only did her reasoning make no sense, but she dropped her eyes and fidgeted. I wasn't going to call her out on it, not yet. But I promised myself that I would get to the bottom of whatever Erica was hiding.

"Okay, Swole kicked my ass," Tammy said, reappearing

at the table with Swole at her side. I mentally cursed them for interrupting our moment.

"And now you owe me twenty bucks," Swole added with a smirk.

"We have a joint bank account," Tammy said. "Taking out the money just to hand it to you would only be symbolic."

"It would symbolize that I'm the Queen of the Pool Table."

"You're so arrogant."

"But you love it," Swole said, throwing an arm over Tammy's shoulders.

"Think one of you can dethrone her majesty here?" Tammy asked.

"I'll try," Erica said.

So, we went to the pool table, and I got to enjoy the view for half an hour as Erica bent at the waist, over and over again. By the time Swole had won the game, I was as hard as a diamond and ready to beg her to wear this damn dress every day.

"Well, it's probably for the best," Erica said as she replaced her pool stick in the holder on the wall. "It's getting late, and I have to go pick up Dominic."

"You sure?" Tammy asked. "Because Heather can keep him longer if you want to stay."

"No, really. He's not used to me going out like this, so I don't want to be gone too long this first time."

"First time?" Tammy smiled. "So, we can expect you to join us again sometime."

"I think so," Erica agreed. She glanced at me before looking back at Tammy. "I had a good time."

"I'll walk you out to your car," I said. We were in Outlaw Souls territory, so she'd probably be fine, but I still didn't like the idea of her walking across the dark parking lot alone.

I grabbed my jacket from my barstool while Erica pulled on her own. I was glad that she had brought one because it was strictly against the rules to let anyone else wear your patch, the only exception being during a ride. If a woman was on the back of your bike, it was acceptable for her to wear it so that your patch, and therefore your membership in the club, could be displayed.

I opened the door for Erica as she waved goodbye to Swole and Tammy. She pointed out where her car was, and the two of us walked side-by-side toward it. I slipped my arm around her waist, letting my fingers curl around her hip. She was so soft pressed against my side.

Erica leaned into me, and we fit together perfectly. When we reached her little red sedan, I stood with my hands in my pockets, waiting for her to dig her keys out of her purse and unlock it. She pushed the button on her key fob, but instead of getting in the car, she hesitated, looking up at me through her eyelashes.

The only light came from a streetlight to the right, which cast half her face in shadow, but I could see exactly what she wanted. One small step closed the distance between us, and I didn't hold back. Taking a fistful of her soft hair, I gave it a small tug, not enough to hurt, but it did make her tilt her head back. I claimed her mouth in a hard kiss, pouring every ounce of desire I had into it as I licked my way into her mouth.

If Erica thought I was being too forward, she didn't show it. In fact, her hands came up to my shoulders, pulling on me until I was even closer, our bodies pressed together. She was intoxicating, so sweet and hot.

I wanted to take this so much further, but I knew that

this wasn't the time. We didn't know each other well, and while I had hopped into bed with women while barely knowing their name, Erica didn't seem like the type to be down with that. She also had her kid to take care of.

I pulled back slightly, breaking the kiss. Letting out a sigh, I rested my forehead against hers. "We'll finish this another time."

"You promise?"

I cupped her cheek, running my thumb over her kiss-bitten lips. "Baby, that's a guarantee."

EIGHT

ERICA

I couldn't stop thinking about kissing Trainer last night. He was rough, the way that I expected, but it didn't cross a line. No, it was just enough to set me on fire.

I wanted more.

It looked like it was time to officially abandon my idea of avoiding the man. I was fighting a losing battle. Every time I saw him, I felt like there was a magnet in the center of my chest, pulling me in his direction.

"Come *on,* we're gonna be late," Dominic waited impatiently by the front door while I pulled on a pair of ankle boots.

"Okay, okay. Don't rush me," I grumbled.

I was never much of a morning person, but how could I say no when Dominic asked me to get up early on my day off to take him to the library's Youth Reading Program? It wasn't an option. I was blessed with a great kid that loved reading, of all things, and was eager to embrace the freedom of our new life. So, I dragged myself out of bed when I would have rather lingered beneath the warm comforter.

We left the house and hit the Starbucks drive-thru

before going to the library. I was surprised by the number of kids there already. Who would have thought that so many kids liked reading enough to come here on a Saturday morning?

There were at least two dozen kids, between the ages of five and ten, all crowded into the kids' room. The main body of the library was standard: neutral walls, tall bookshelves, and a quiet atmosphere. But the kids' room was an explosion of color. The carpet was a deep blue, while the walls were a cheery yellow. There were paper mache planets, suns, and moons hanging from the ceiling, which I thought might be a part of some kind of art program offered by the library. Even the books were all an array of colors.

One of the librarians was bringing bean bag chairs out of a closet and scattering them over the floor for the kids to sit on. Dominic lingered by my side for a few minutes, as the other kids interacted. They had probably been coming to this bi-weekly reading program for a long time, and all knew each other.

"Hi, I'm Dave," a man beside me spoke.

"Erica," I responded. I was getting used to using my fake name. I hardly had to think about it now.

There was a little girl at his side, but she was quick to hurry forward and join the others. "Wait a minute, Stacey. Why don't you take our new friend here over to meet everyone."

She came back, boldly grabbing Dominic's hand and pulling him into the thick of things. I chuckled as he looked back at me with wide eyes, but it didn't take long for him to join the others, introducing himself and claiming a beanbag chair as his own.

"Thanks for that," I said.

"I know how it is. Not always easy to meet new people."

"And it gets even harder as you get older," I agreed.

"I think that depends on the person," he said, his voice deepening as he leaned a little closer to me.

Is he hitting on me?

There was something familiar about Dave. He was tall and classically handsome with his clean-shaven jaw and crew-cut blonde hair. He was... smooth. Confident. Those sounded like good qualities, but unease gripped me.

Then, I realized. He reminded me of Jeff.

"They're starting," he said, nodding to the group children as the head librarian passed out copies of the book they would be reading together. They all settled onto bean bags, their rapt attention on the woman seated before them. All the parents filed out of the room, some heading straight for the exit, others lingering to chat quietly. "It'll be at least a half an hour before they're done. Do you want to go grab a coffee, maybe get to know each other better?"

Dave flashed what he probably thought was a charming grin, but it fell flat for me.

"I already have one," I held up the frappuccino I had picked up on the way to the library. "Thanks anyway."

Luckily, he took the hint and didn't press the issue. As Dave made his way out of the library, I looked around, getting lost among the shelves. I was a fan of true crime, and they had a whole section that I spent time perusing, but I didn't have a library card, and I wasn't sure if I would need identification to get one.

Only fifteen minutes had passed, so I made my way outside for some fresh air. It was a perfect spring day, with a cloudless blue sky and the sun shining overhead. The leaves in the trees were new and green, and dandelions were starting to pop up in the grass. There were metal benches lined up along the sidewalk, and I took a seat on one.

I looked around, taking note of the Methodist church across the street and the community center a block away. There was a flower shop next to the church and a gas station by the library. As I looked that way, my eyes landed on a motorcycle parked at the gas station. My heart lurched as I realized that I recognized that bike.

The door of the gas station opened, and the man that had been running through my mind appeared, opening a candy bar. Trainer was dressed as usual in his leather jacket, black t-shirt, and worn jeans with a pair of cuffed up riding boots. The sight of my big biker man indulging in chocolate of all things made a goofy smile stretch across my face.

The gas station wasn't far from the library, and he happened to have parked on the edge of the parking lot closest to me, so it wasn't a surprise when he spotted me watching him. I didn't even try to pretend that I wasn't staring, just lifting my hand and waving at him.

Trainer looked at me, then at his candy bar before shoving the thing into the pocket of his jacket, still half-eaten. I could swear that he almost looked embarrassed, which had me giggling as he bypassed the motorcycle and walked over to me.

"What's so funny?" he growled, but his eyes held amusement.

"That chocolate bar is going to melt."

"Oh, hell," he pulled it out of his pocket, pulling the wrapper back once again, and I saw that it was a Snickers. "You want a bite?"

I wrinkled my nose, "No, thanks. I'm not a big fan of nuts."

"How unfortunate," he said, taking a big bite and wiggling his eyebrows. I slapped his arm playfully. "So...

this is how you spend your Saturday mornings," he looked around thoughtfully. "Nice enough spot to sit, I suppose."

"Please," I rolled my eyes. "I'd much rather be at home, wearing pajamas and eating cereal in front of the TV."

"It's almost ten o'clock."

"Yeah, and I like sleeping in," I pinned him with a fierce glare. "Don't you judge me."

"I had no idea you were so defensive," Trainer grinned.

"You're supposed to be intimidated."

"Oh. My bad." He rolled his eyes and took a seat on the bench beside me. "So, what dragged you out of bed against your will?"

"Dominic. He's nuts about reading, always has been, and he somehow found out that this library has a youth reading program every other Saturday."

"Reading, huh? How old is he?"

"Seven."

"Damn. At that age, I was obsessed with video games. I had an original Nintendo, which was outdated even then, but I took really good care of it. I was on that thing all the time."

I loved the image that his words conjured in my mind. A little boy with dark hair sitting on the floor in front of the TV with a controller in his hand, working his way through the classic games.

"Dominic likes video games too. I mean, what kid doesn't? It's funny that you mention the old game system since he's been using a Gameboy that I've had since I was little. Once I get a few more paychecks, I think I'll get him a system he can play at home on the TV."

"Sounds like he's lucky to have you."

Warmth filled my chest. How many times had Jeff told

me that I was a horrible mother? Too many to count. It was hard not to believe his words sometimes.

I had to stop doing that. Thinking about Jeff and the shit he put me through wasn't helping me move on, and it mentally took me away from the intriguing man in front of me. My focus should be on him alone.

"Thanks," I said. My eye caught on something on the front of his jacket. Looking closer, I saw that it was another patch that had been sewn on. It was diamond-shaped and inside was "1%".

Trainer followed my gaze, "Wondering about the one percent patch?" I nodded. "It's part of being an outlaw motorcycle club. Basically, we aren't a part of the ninety-nine percent of clubs that belong to the AMA."

"Outlaw?" I wasn't too sure I liked the sound of that.

"It's meant to refer to the fact that we aren't an AMA sanctioned group, but..."

"But you guys do illegal stuff?"

"There's not a good way to answer that," he admitted.

I wasn't sure that I actually wanted him to, but wasn't it reckless of me to keep this thing going with him if I didn't ask?

"Let me put it this way," he continued, "we've broken the law. The club has a history of doing some bad things. But we've turned it around... for the most part. These days we try to do better for the community."

"That's good."

I noticed that he didn't say that they were no longer lawbreakers. I wanted to press him for details, but I didn't think I would get them. I was no expert on motorcycle clubs, but I figured they were probably pretty secretive. So, I had to decide if I could accept that the Outlaw Souls - and by extension, Trainer - were probably involved in some questionable activities.

I studied him for a long moment, and he met my eyes directly, not shying away or hiding. I felt like I could see him clearly for who he was, and I knew that I was looking at a good man. That was what really mattered, right?

Someone might look at Trainer and have doubts about him because of the patch on the back of his jacket or his large stature, but that stuff didn't really tell you anything. It made me think of Jeff. He was always well put-together, fitting in well with the high society types that he associated with. But on the inside, he was a monster.

Damn it. Was I ever going to stop thinking about him?

I didn't know what to say to Trainer to let him know that I was okay with what he told me, so I reached out and took his hand. I hadn't realized that he was tense until I did that, and I saw him relax. We sat there quietly for a while, and it was nice to just relax with him like this without feeling like I needed to fill the air with endless chatter.

The door of the library opened, and I turned, releasing Trainer's hand. Dominic stepped out, looking far too worried. I hadn't seen him with that look on his face since we moved here, and guilt flooded me. I should have realized that he'd be freaked out if he couldn't find me. It probably brought up some stuff from the past that I didn't want him to dwell on.

"Hey, buddy," I stood. "I just stepped out for some fresh air. Are you all done in there?"

"Yeah," he said, all concern disappearing as if it had never been there at all. "We read a book about elves." He looked quizzically at Trainer, "Who are you?"

"Trainer," he walked forward and held his large hand

out. Dominic took it, looking suspicious. "I'm a friend of your mom's."

This was not how I would have had them meet. Actually, I hadn't even started to consider how or when to introduce Dominic to a man I was dating. Until recently, I had no real plans to date at all.

Dominic turned to me with puppy dog eyes as Trainer released his hand. "Mom, can I go to Glenn's house? Please?"

"Who's Glenn?"

A woman had just stepped out of the library, and she smiled brightly at me when she heard my question. "That would be my son. Elaine Hargrave, nice to meet you."

She stepped closer, like she was going to shake my hand, but stopped when she saw Trainer. Elaine's emotions were printed across her face, and I saw apprehension there. She seemed immediately unsettled, and I had the urge to defend Trainer, to tell her that he was nothing to be afraid of.

"I'm Erica, and this is my friend, Trainer."

Elaine refocused on me, "It seems that our boys have hit it off."

I looked at Dominic and saw that another little boy had come outside and joined him. They were in the middle of an animated discussion about Spider-man.

"We'd love to have a playdate. I can take the boys to mine for the afternoon. Glenn is always looking for friends to share his love of comic books with."

"Can I go, mom?"

I felt almost like a cornered animal as I looked from one hopeful face to the next. My instinct was to say no. I just couldn't think of a good reason on the spot like this. I didn't even know this woman, how could I trust her with my child?

"It would be no problem, really," Elaine assured me. "I'll give you my phone number so we can coordinate pick up later."

"Well..." I had to put my fear of people behind me. "Okay."

"Yes!" Dominic and Glenn both cried out.

"Fabulous," Elaine said, pulling out her cell phone. "Tell me your number, and I'll text you so that you have mine."

As I rattled off the digits, I could feel Trainer watching me as if he could sense my distress about this situation. He stayed on the bench as I grabbed Dominic's booster seat from the car and put it into Elaine's minivan, which was conveniently parked beside me. I stood at the curb and watched them drive off before returning to him, practically collapsing on to the bench once again.

"You know, you could have said no," he told me, confirming my suspicions about his perception of my feelings.

"And Dominic would have been heartbroken," I shook my head. "He was so excited to make a new friend, and he deserves some good in his life."

"What do you mean by that?"

I cast my gaze around, searching for a way to change the subject since I couldn't seem to keep my big mouth closed. It landed on his bike.

"Would you take me for a ride? I've never been on a motorcycle before."

Trainer didn't respond right away, and I was worried that he wasn't going to let it go, insisting that I explain my comment about Dominic. But after a few seconds, he stood and held his hand out to me.

"Never been on a motorcycle? That should be a crime."

I held his hand as we walked the short distance to his Harley, our fingers intertwined. When we reached the bike, I was surprised by how tall it was. It didn't look so high up from further away. I was average height, but I wouldn't even be able to skim the ground with my toes if I sat on it.

Trainer grabbed a hold of the handlebars and raised the kickstand before swinging one leg over the side. When both of his feet were flat on either side of the machine, he turned to look at me.

"Put this on." Taking his helmet off of the seat behind him, Trainer handed it over. I could tell already that it was going to be too big.

"It won't fit."

"I know, but it's better than nothing. I'll get you your own for the future."

The future. It should probably scare me that he was making plans like that, considering my situation. I might have to run away again at a moment's notice. But I didn't feel scared at his words. A glimmer of hope sparked within my heart, and I shoved the helmet onto my head, tightening the strap as much as possible. It was still a little loose, but not too bad. I wanted to protest his lack of head protection, but I had a feeling it would fall on deaf ears. There was no way that a man like Trainer would allow me to go without a helmet so that he could have one.

Reaching up, I held onto his shoulders and placed my foot on the passenger footrest before hoisting my body off the ground and onto the motorcycle. Settling into the seat behind him, I felt my core clench as my thighs had to spread wide to fit on each side of his body. My chest was pressed against his back as I leaned forward, wrapping my arms around his waist.

Trainer fired up the bike, the growl of the engine

making me jump. I settled down quickly, resting my head against his shoulder blade. When he pulled out of the parking lot, he turned left, passing by the front of the library just as Dave emerged with his daughter. We made eye contact, and I smiled as his jaw dropped.

Then, Trainer shifted gears, and we were gone.

NINE
TRAINER

I didn't usually ride with people on the back of my bike. It wasn't a hard rule, but riding with a passenger changed the balancing and made me responsible for someone else's safety. I wasn't a big fan of either of those things.

But I didn't think I could deny Erica anything. The more time I spent with her, the more I could see glimpses of vulnerability beneath the surface that made me want to take care of her. So, if she wanted to experience the thrill of a ride, I'd give it to her.

I noticed right away that turning made her nervous. Her entire body stiffened up behind me when I leaned into a turn, and her arms tightened to the point of almost hurting. Not wanting to make this a nerve-wracking experience for her, I headed to western La Playa. There was a straight stretch of road that ran along the beach. It was a bit boring for riding, with no twists or turns, but I thought she might enjoy the view.

The sun shone brightly off the sand, making me thankful for my sunglasses. I felt Erica relax against me, even her arms loosened their death-grip, moving lower on my abdomen. An erotic excitement sparked, and I wanted her touch on my bare skin, moving lower and lower until she gripped my throbbing erection.

Okay, time to take a break.

We'd been driving for almost an hour anyway. It would be good to stretch our legs. I pulled over as we came upon the boardwalk. It was the most popular tourist attraction in La Playa with a Ferris wheel, carnival-style games, a family pavilion, and a stage where bands often performed on the weekend evenings.

The place was crawling with people, so I made sure that Erica stayed close to my side as we walked along the wooden planks.

"I had no idea this was here," she commented, her gaze on the ocean. "Do you come here often?"

"Nah, it's usually too crowded for me, too many tourists."

"I kind of like it."

"I thought you might."

We passed a caricaturist drawing three sisters as they posed with their heads pressed together and a little boy with his dad flying a drone over all our heads. Finally, I spotted a pretzel cart ahead.

"In the mood for lunch?" I asked, pointing it out to her. It was no gourmet meal, but I thought it was best to keep things real with her. I was never going to be a fine-dining kind of guy.

Erica didn't mind. She pulled me over to the cart, taking her time picking out the "perfect pretzel."

I wasn't aware that such a thing existed, but she was almost scientific about it. Apparently, the amount and distribution of salt really mattered in these decisions. Me? I just pointed to the first one I saw and asked for extra cheese sauce.

"I think that thing is bigger than your head," I told Erica as we took a seat at a small, metal cafe-style table nearby.

"The bigger, the better," she said. Her eyes widened as the words left her mouth, and she glanced down at my lap. My erection twitched, as if begging for more of her attention. She bit her lip, and I groaned.

"Don't do that," I said, reaching out to gently tug her lip out from between her teeth. "Not here."

"Why?"

"It's too sexy."

And now she blushed, the pink tint of her cheeks evidence of a sweetness that was driving me crazy. I wasn't used to spending much time with a woman before taking her to bed. Casual flings were really only about one thing.

"I don't know if I've ever had a man look at me like you are right now," she said, a little breathlessly.

"And how's that?" I asked, leaning closer to her across the table. Our pretzels were laying in their paper sheaths between us, all but forgotten.

"Like you need me. Like you'll starve without me."

That was a hell of a way of putting it. But she was right.

Before I got the chance to respond, I picked up something in my peripheral vision that distracted me. It was a biker, but I didn't recognize him. Which meant that he was probably a Las Balas member. Or a Prospect.

My attention wasn't just drawn by the man's attire. It was his behavior. He looked shifty, his eyes darting around as he bounced on the balls of his feet. He didn't seem to be able to hold still. The guy was definitely on something. Based on the way that he kept checking his pockets and clenching his jaw, I assumed he was holding and anxious about it from the drug use. A dealer maybe?

Someone should have told him not to take his own shit. It was bad for business.

"What are you looking at?" Erica asked, turning to look in the same direction.

"No, don't look," I commanded, my voice coming out harsher than intended. The guy looked way too jumpy, and if he caught on to being watched, things could get ugly. I was packing, of course, but I didn't really want to get into a public fight with a rival gang member.

No, this would have to be handled with some finesse. I needed to talk to Ryder.

"What's wrong?" Erica's question came out as more of a demand for an answer, and I smirked.

"It's kind of club business, but I'll tell you that there's a guy to our left, next to the beer garden, that looks like trouble to me. Maybe a drug dealer. I just don't want you to turn your head his way too because it will be too obvious. This guy looks like the unstable type to me."

"A drug dealer? Should we call the police?" To my surprise, she didn't sound too keen on the idea herself.

I shook my head from side to side. "No. We handle this."

"*We*? You mean the Outlaw Souls?"

"Yes."

Erica didn't say anything else, just turning her attention to the pretzel. I watched her pick pieces off of it, nibbling on them with a troubled look on her face.

"You want to tell me what's wrong? Does it bother you that I won't call the cops?"

"No," she said, meeting my eyes. In the sunlight, her

vivid green orbs were even more entrancing than usual. "I just... I don't like the idea of you in dangerous situations."

The woman couldn't seem to stop astounding me. She was worried about me?

"Don't worry about me. The Outlaw Souls have each other's backs. They're pretty much the only family I have."

"Really?"

"Well, there's my foster mother, Mama Tammy. She insists that I call her that."

"You were a foster child? What happened to your parents?"

"Dad was never around. Mom was a mess. I was taken from her when I was twelve, and I haven't had contact with her since." I kept it short, not wanting to rehash my tragic backstory. There was no point in lingering in the past. "What about you? You have a good relationship with your parents?"

"No, they died when I was eighteen. It was a fire at the house. I was still living with them, but that night I had gone to an overnight college orientation, so I wasn't there." her voice cracked, and I thought I saw tears in her eyes, but they didn't fall down her cheeks. "Maybe if I had been, I could've helped them."

"You don't know that," I argued. "You could've gone with them, and I'm sure they wouldn't have wanted that."

"I know," she nodded, but the pain was still etched in her features. "But they were my only family, and I feel like I let them down."

I regretted asking about her parents. It was a real shit situation, what happened to her. It was worse than my circumstances, in my opinion. I never had parents to care about, not really. So I didn't feel like I lost anything, even when I went into the system. You couldn't lose what you never had. But Erica had to deal with the sudden loss of people that she loved at such a young age. That kind of thing changed a person.

"No other family?" I knew how that was. "What about Dominic's dad? Where is he?"

It was something that I had been wondering about since I found out there was a kid in the picture. I wasn't intimidated by the idea of a jealous ex, but I also didn't like to compete for affection. If Dominic's dad still held a piece of her heart, I'd rather know now.

Erica's demeanor completely changed, when I mentioned the mystery man. Before, she'd been sad, but open. Now, she was completely closed off. Her back went ramrod straight, and all emotion was wiped from her face. I'd never seen someone put on a mask so quickly.

"He's no one. He's not in the picture."

Well, it looked like sharing time was over. I let the subject drop, but one day she'd have to tell me what she was hiding. I didn't care if she'd done something bad, I was in no place to judge, but I didn't think that was it. She was haunted by something in her past.

"He seems like a good kid," I said. "You've got this single parent thing down. That's all a kid needs, at least one person that gives a damn. Mama Tammy was that person for me."

We'd finished our pretzels and were once again walking along the boardwalk. There were people all around, but I felt like it was just the two of us. She held my complete attention.

"You guys are still in touch?"

"Yeah. I moved out as soon as I turned eighteen, but I try to visit her every Sunday."

"That's nice."

Erica's phone beeped, and she checked the text message. "Looks like Elaine is ready for me to pick up Dominic."

"Let's go."

When we got back to the bike, I mounted it and waited for her to climb up. A she settled in behind me, an unfamiliar feeling also settled in the center of my chest. A feeling of rightness and affection that I wasn't quite ready to examine closely. All I knew right now was that I had the right girl on the back of my bike for the first time ever.

TEN
ERICA

Monday was the beginning of my second week at the fitness center. I was fortunate in that yoga was very popular in this area, so I usually had a couple of classes a day. I wasn't exactly rolling in the dough, but at least I had food in the fridge, and my rent was going to be paid on time.

I had even started to do research into different styles of yoga, such as prenatal and silent. I quickly discarded anything involving animals, such as cats, rabbits, and… goats? People had some strange ideas, but I didn't think any kind of furry creature would be a good idea inside the gym. I wouldn't want to clean up any messes afterward.

I wanted to offer a bigger variety to draw in more students and make myself a vital part of the team here. The first thing I wanted to add to the class schedule was a Mommy and Me class. It appealed to the parent side of me, and I thought that it would be a fun way to include Dominic in this part of my life.

I pitched the idea to Swole when she came by to check in with me before my last class of the day.

"Hmm, that's interesting," she crossed her arms and tilted her head to the side as her eyes took on a faraway look. "An evening class, I think. Start with one mid-week. We could emphasize the importance of youth fitness and maybe offer some kind of a discount if kids sign up for our new kids gymnastics classes."

Swole was clearly talking to herself, working out the logistics in the way that an experienced manager does, but I couldn't help interrupting.

"Gymnastic classes?"

"Yeah. Since Emory is getting older, I've been learning what a money pit kids are, and I figured it would be a good idea for the gym to benefit from it."

I laughed. She had that right.

Swole left as my students started to file into the room for their beginner's yoga class, promising to get back to me soon about the Mommy and Me class. I could tell she liked the idea, and that made me feel good because I respected the woman. She was smart and tough. No one would ever cross her. If I were more like that, I wouldn't have become a battered wife.

As I rolled out my yoga mat and turned on soothing music, I told myself to focus on the now. All I could do was try to be a stronger woman now.

The class lasted an hour, and it was five in the evening by the time we were finished. I had arranged a daily pick-up time of six o'clock with Jennifer. This allowed me time to clean up and shower without hurrying. When I stepped out of the yoga room, I was looking at the main body of the gym, with rows of various exercise equipment on blue mats. Monday wasn't the fitness center's busiest day, being the beginning of many people's workweek and all, so the place was nearly empty. There were two men on weight machines and a woman, with earbuds in, was running full-out on a treadmill. I could hear a rhythmic thumping from near the locker rooms, but that wasn't within my line of vision.

Pulling out my cell phone, I checked for text messages. I kept it on vibrate during classes, and I wanted to make sure I hadn't missed anything from Dominic's sitter, Tammy, or Trainer.

Okay, I was mostly hoping to hear from Trainer.

But there was nothing. I frowned and shoved the thing back into my gym bag as I headed to the locker room. I rounded a corner and saw the source of the thumping. My mouth went dry as I watched Trainer working on a punching bag, beating the crap out of it. His body was channeling more power than I would have thought possible as he threw punch after punch at the heavy bag, making the chains that connected it the floor and ceiling rattle.

He hadn't seen me yet. His concentration was so fierce on the punching bag. There was something hostile in his expression. Something was wrong.

Before I could decide how to approach him, Trainer pivoted around the punching bag on the balls of his feet. His arms were still raised to continue throwing punches, but when he saw me standing there, he froze. His big body was unmoving except for his chest that pumped up and down with his heavy breaths. His eyes widened slightly as he took me in.

"Uh, I didn't mean to interrupt-"

I stopped speaking as he took a step toward me. That menacing quality I sensed before remained, and I had the vague thought that I should be afraid, but I wasn't. Instead, I wanted him more than ever.

Trainer stalked across the blue mat beneath our feet,

not stopping until barely an inch of space separated us. I could feel the heat radiating from his body, warming my own. I tilted my head back to look up into his face. He looked less angry, but there was a lingering darkness that I wanted to make disappear.

Trainer ran the tips of his fingers up my arm, the barely-there touch leaving behind goosebumps. "Meet me outside in ten minutes."

I couldn't seem to breathe, so I just nodded. Trainer pecked my lips before stepping around me, and went into the Men's locker room. I stood there for a beat, in a daze. Then, I snapped out of it and hurried into the Women's locker room.

While showering, I tried not to linger on my most sensitive parts. My nipples were hardened nubs, and my clit felt swollen. Images of Trainer's muscled body ran through my mind.

I was outside in exactly ten minutes, with my wet hair pulled back with a hair tie. I stepped out into the parking lot, looking around until I spotted him already waiting for me, leaning against my car. As I drew closer to him, the smell of sandalwood reached me.

Once I was within arms reach, Trainer dragged my body into his, crushing my mouth with his own. I melted into him, surrendering as he took what he wanted... what we both needed. By the time he pulled away, I was yearning for more.

"Do you have time?" he asked. I checked my phone. Five-Twenty. I showed Trainer.

"I have to pick up Dominic at six."

He nodded. "Not enough time. But I have to have a taste." Trainer took my car keys out of my hand and got into the driver seat. "Get in the back."

I did, and Trainer started up the car, only to drive it around to the back of the building, out of sight of the road. He parked next to a metal door with an EXIT sign hanging above it. I looked around. With the position of the large dumpster and the L-shape of the building, we had as much privacy as possible here. As Trainer put the car in park and climbed into the backseat with me, I felt a small thrill at the knowledge that we were technically in public. It might be unlikely, but we could get caught, and that reality made my lust surge forward.

When Trainer had the door closed behind him, I boldly straddled him and pressed my lips to his once again. The hard evidence of his desire pressed against me, creating a glorious friction as I rubbed myself back and forth against him. Trainer's hands landed on my hips before going underneath my shirt. His calloused hands against my bare back made a shiver travel down my spine.

"So fucking soft," he murmured as he broke our kiss to trail kisses across my cheek and down my neck. His beard was soft against my skin.

I reached down to grab the hem of my shirt and pull it over my head. The red satin bra I had just put on had a front clasp, so I opened it. Trainer wasted no time leaning forward and taking a nipple into his mouth while bringing his hand forward to cup my other breast.

I gasped as he sucked lightly on my nipple, sending waves of pleasure straight to the juncture between my thighs. My hands went to his hair as he switched to my other breast, giving it the same lavish attention.

By now, my hips were thrusting wildly as I searched for a release, but it wasn't enough. I needed more of him than the outline of his erection in his jeans.

"Trainer..." I didn't know how to put my need into

words, but he seemed to understand. Moving me as if I were weightless, Trainer sat me sideways onto the seat with my back pressed up against the door.

Trainer crouched down in front of me, somehow cramming his big body onto the rest of the backseat. It couldn't have been comfortable, but he didn't seem to care at all. As his hands trailed up my legs, the heated look in his eyes said that he was exactly where he wanted to be.

I had never been so happy to be wearing a skirt in my life. In fact, I was seriously considering trading in every pair of jeans I owned for more skirts and dresses so that he could always have easy access.

Trainer's lips left a trail of kisses along my inner thigh as he pushed my skirt up around my waist. Lifting my legs, he threw them over his shoulders, angling my hips in just the right way to allow him full access to my pussy. Pulling my panties to the side, he licked up my center, drawing a long moan from my lips.

Trainer was talented. There was no doubt about that. As he buried his face between my legs, I came undone. Legs shaking, I groaned and cried out in pleasure. He built up my ecstasy higher and higher until I was right on the edge of completion.

"Trainer, please... I need more," my voice was breathless and needy.

Flicking my clit with his tongue, Trainer inserted a single, thick finger inside of me.

That was it. My orgasm slammed into me, and I found myself calling out his name like a prayer while I thrust my hands into his hair, pulling his face closer. Trainer lapped at me, taking his time as I rode out the climax.

Finally, I collapsed against the door, feeling boneless.

Trainer lifted his head and looked at me with a wicked grin. My heart skittered as I saw the satisfaction in his face. This man had just given me the best orgasm of my life, and he was looking at me like I had given *him* a gift.

Who knew that men like this existed?

ELEVEN

TRAINER

I had a shitty day right up until I saw Erica. When I looked up from the punching bag I was punishing, everything seemed to turn on a dime. The aggression I was wrestling with, born of the helpless feeling I had, in the face of Mama Tammy's potential illness, shifted into something else. It burned just as hot as anger, but was far more satisfying.

Now, sitting in the backseat of her small car with my arm around her shoulders and her taste still on my tongue, I was relaxed for the first time since I woke up this morning.

"You want to tell me what's going on with you?" she asked, her voice quiet.

I glanced at the time. Fifteen minutes until she had to pick up Dominic. We needed to part ways soon.

I took a deep breath and let it out slowly. "You remember when I told you about Mama Tammy?"

"Your foster mom? Yeah, I remember."

"She had a biopsy done today. I took her."

"A biopsy?"

"I guess she has a lump. The doctor isn't sure if it's something to worry about, so he took a piece to test."

Erica lifted her head off my chest, looking into my face with her brow furrowed. "I'm sorry."

"Yeah." I was worried as hell, but I wasn't sure I wanted to talk about it, even with her. "It's a bad deal, and I can't do shit about it except wait to hear some news."

"It bothers you not having someone or something to fight." It wasn't a question. We had known each other for such a short period of time, but she already knew me well.

I grunted.

"Okay, Mr. Tough Guy. I get it. We don't have to talk about it. In fact," she checked her phone for the time. "I need to get going."

I clenched my jaw, but didn't argue. I got it, she had to get her kid. But a part of me wanted to go with her. To maybe get to know the boy because he was so important to her, and I might want to be a lasting part of her life.

But those thoughts scared me.

I'd done the solo thing for most of my life, not always by choice. Sure, I had the Outlaw Souls, but they were all tough as nails, people that I didn't have to worry about. Then, there was Mama Tammy. Look at how the idea of her having cancer was tearing me up, and I didn't even know if it was true yet. Did I really want to go further into this thing with Erica, knowing that I'd have the added weight of concern for her and Dominic on my shoulders? Was the burden of that worth the payoff? Looking into her face, I wanted to say yes, but I was also smart enough to know that caring came with risk to the heart.

I shook my head at myself. When did I become such a chicken shit?

Almost to prove to myself that I wasn't, I leaned forward and pressed a quick, hard kiss to Erica's mouth. She gave as good as she got, and I broke it off too soon. It was never enough with her. We both got out of the car.

"Call me. Or text. Whatever." She smiled as she pulled her car door open. "But next time we get together, it's your turn."

Fuck.

"Can't wait," I said honestly. The very thought of her plump lips wrapped around my cock was enough to drive me mad.

I stood back from the car and watched her drive away before walking around the building to where my bike was parked. I didn't expect these conflicting feelings. Hadn't I just been lamenting my jealousy of people I knew in good, lasting relationships? I should be nothing but happy to have found a woman I might want that with. Instead, I was playing out hypotheticals in my head.

What if she got sick or hurt? What if she lost interest in me?

Like my mom did.

Damn it. I needed a drink.

Luckily, there was a pretty great bar right across the street.

I WOKE up the next day to my cell phone ringing. Fumbling around with my eyes still closed, I knocked it off my nightstand, making me crack my eyelids open to find it on the floor. Ryder's name on the screen had me answering immediately, even though my voice was a harsh croak.

"Meeting at the bar in an hour." Ryder hung up before I could reply, but that didn't matter. It wasn't a request.

Sitting up in bed, I stretched my arms over my head,

feeling my back crack. Cramming myself into the backseat of that car last night had not been easy or comfortable, and I was paying for it today, but it was worth it. My morning erection throbbed at the memory of Erica's moans and the way she'd gasped my name.

I still wasn't sure what I wanted out of this relationship with her, but my body had plenty of ideas about it. I was yawning as I stumbled into the bathroom, tripping over my damn boot that I had kicked off the night before.

Righting myself, I headed to the shower and turned it on the hottest temperature I could stand. Shedding my boxers, I stepped under the spray, letting the warmth seep into my muscles and relax them. My shower at the gym last night had been a quick one, since I was so eager to get outside to meet Erica. This morning I took my time, washing every inch of my body slowly. My skin felt overly sensitive, and the erection jutting out at my hips wasn't going away any time soon.

Finally, I decided that I'd have to do something about it. Leaning my back against the tiled wall of the shower, I gripped myself. A fantasy played out in my mind of Erica here with me, water droplets running down her naked body as she got on her knees. I remembered the way her eyes seemed to turn a darker shade of green when she was aroused, and I imagined her looking up at me through her eyelashes with that same raw heat. I wanted it to be her hand on me... her lips... her tight-

My orgasm rippled through me faster than I expected, and Erica's name left my lips with a low moan. The evidence of my release washed down the drain, as I stood there trying to slow my racing heart.

One thing was clear: I needed more of Erica.

When I was done showering, I hurried through my

morning routine and left the house ten minutes later. When I reached the bar, the parking lot was already half-full of motorcycles.

Our two Prospects, Denny and Blade, were flanking the door of the bar, ensuring that no one came in during our meeting other than Outlaw Souls members. I nodded to both men as I passed.

The front of the bar was desert, with chairs still up on the tables from mopping the night before. It wouldn't open for several more hours. I headed to the backroom, where all the meetings were held. I could hear the voices of the members that were already waiting.

It looked like I was the last to arrive as I pushed open the door and everyone looked my way. Ryder stood up as I planted myself in the closest empty seat I saw.

"Alright. Now that we're all here, I'll get right to it." He looked angry. "You all know that we've been tracking an increase in meth in the community. Well, thanks to Trainer spotting a dealer down by the boardwalk, we've officially been able to link it to Las Balas."

"So, what are we going to do about it?" Moves asked. As our enforcer, he was always eager to go bust some heads.

"There's a bigger problem. In our surveillance of the dealer, we discovered that we'd been betrayed by one of our own."

"What do you mean?" I asked.

"Carlos. He's been spying on us for Las Balas for months," Ryder spoke through gritted teeth.

"Why?" Pin asked. I could hear my confusion reflected in his voice. Carlos was our friend, a part of the MC family. I couldn't understand how he could do such a thing.

"It's the bullshit drug," Ryder explained. "He's a meth head. I missed the signs-"

"We all did," Swole cut in. She was the only one that didn't appear shocked by this. I figured she helped Ryder *interrogate* Carlos. How else could they have acquired this information?

"Yeah, well," Ryder scanned each of our faces, as if he were looking for a sign of disloyalty. He wouldn't find one in me. "The point is, Carlos Brown has been banned from the club, and if anyone sees him in our territory again, let me know immediately."

"I doubt he'll be stupid enough to come around," Swole said, cracking her knuckles. "That broken jaw of his should be a hell of a reminder that we aren't to be trifled with."

"All the same," Ryder said. "La Balas have crossed a line by converting one of our patches. As far as I'm concerned, they've declared war."

TWELVE
ERICA

I felt like I hadn't spent any quality time with Dominic lately. Maybe it was some form of separation anxiety since I had a job now. I felt like I was missing a connection with him. He spent more time with the babysitter than with me.

So, when I picked him up from the sitter this evening, I didn't take us home. Instead, we went to the pizza place for his favorite dinner. As Dominic sat opposite me in the booth, filling me in on his day, it struck me that this place already felt like home. We'd been here for two weeks and had started to build a life.

I just prayed that we would be able to stay.

"Mom?" Dominic suddenly looked pensive as he dropped his eyes.

"What is it?" I reached out and put my hand over his own.

"Do you think dad's going to find us?"

My blood ran cold at the fear in his voice. How long would the memory of the things Jeff had done, haunt my little boy?

He'd never hit Dominic. I made sure of that. If he'd

seemed like he might try, I always redirected his anger to me. It was worth it, but it didn't protect Dominic from seeing me be slapped around. I was sure that he'd also heard some pretty terrible arguing, with horrible things being said.

"I don't know," I told him honestly. "But I will always do whatever I can to keep you safe."

"Who's going to keep you safe?"

His question made me grimace. I didn't want him to worry about me, but what could I say?

Absurdly, I thought of Trainer. Big and strong, he'd be able to fill the role of protector, but there was no reason to think that he'd want to. There was something between us, a sexual attraction, maybe even more, but that didn't mean he would want to take on my baggage.

I had to depend on myself.

"Don't worry about me," I told him. "Things are different now. We don't live with him."

Dominic looked thoughtful for a moment. "Maybe we should get a dog."

"Oh, you do?" I smiled. He'd asked for one before, but Jeff would never allow an animal into his house.

"Not for a pet," he clarified. "A guard dog."

I opened my mouth to tell him that we didn't need a guard dog, but the hopeful expression on his face stopped me. If it would make him feel safer, why not? I knew that the landlord would allow it, he'd had the property listed as pet-friendly.

"Okay," I said, and Dominic's entire face lit up. "We'll go get one tomorrow."

After dinner, we went to a movie at the theater located inside the mall. It was billed as a kid's movie, and it was animated, but I enjoyed it. The company was the best part. Between the two of us, we demolished a large bucket of popcorn, and I felt like I was going to explode by the time we left the theater.

As we walked across the mall, heading to the entrance, I spotted Trainer coming out of a store with a man that I didn't recognize but knew to be an Outlaw Soul by the patch on the back of his jacket. I wanted to call out to him, but the sight of another person stopped me. Unfortunately, Dominic didn't feel the same.

"Hey, isn't that your friend Trainer?" he said loudly, pointing.

Trainer's head whipped around. Seeing us, he mumbled something I couldn't hear to the man beside him and headed our way.

"Hey, little man," he said, ruffling Dominic's hair. "What are you guys up to?"

"What just saw a movie-" I started, but Dominic cut me off excitedly.

"Mom said we could get a dog!"

"Yeah, that too." I chuckled. "I'm thinking we'll go to the shelter tomorrow after I get off work."

"I have to wait all day?" Dominic whined.

"'Fraid so."

"It'll be worth it," Trainer assured him. "Actually, I was going to see if you wanted to have dinner together tomorrow night. How about I come with you guys to the shelter, and we can pick up some takeout afterward?"

He wanted to spend time with me *and* Dominic. This felt big, like a significant step in this relationship. We'd never talked about where things were going between us, but his suggestion made it seem that we were moving forward.

A small voice in the back of my mind told me not to do this, not to get attached. Wasn't that the plan? I was going to lay low here for now and figure out my next move when I thought that Jeff had probably given up finding us.

But I found that I wanted to say yes despite all of that. It shifted things to a more serious level, and I wanted to see how far it would go. I wanted him to be mine. Maybe Dominic and I wouldn't have to move on at all.

"Okay," I said. "How about I pick you up after I get off work?"

"Great. I'll be at Ortega's Auto. I've got to go now, but I'll see you then."

Leaning close, he pressed a chaste kiss to my cheek before going to join his friend that was waiting nearby. I looked at Dominic, to see if he had any reaction to Trainer's kiss, but he didn't appear to be bothered by it.

"I can't wait until tomorrow," he said, as we resumed walking to the exit. "Do you think that we should get a puppy or a grown-up dog? They might not have puppies, but that's okay. Do you think the dog will like us? I have so many dog name ideas. Will he have his name already?"

Dominic talked endlessly about the dog as we crossed the parking lot to our car. I let him, my mind a million miles away. Trainer had to know that Dominic and I were a package deal, so the outcome of tomorrow would determine if there was any future for us at all.

DOMINIC WAS LOSING HIS MIND. We were at the shelter, and his excitement level had skyrocketed as he went from one cage to the other, trying to make an impossible decision. I was pretty sure that he'd take them all if I let him.

There were far more dogs here than I had anticipated,

and it broke my heart a little to see it. The shelter was a nice place, and the worker helping us had told me that it had been built just three years ago, with money donated by a local organization that I suspected might be the Outlaw Souls based on Trainer's subtle fidgeting. But this was still no place for a dog to live. They should be in homes with yards and loving families.

"Mom, look at this one," Dominic called, pointing into a cage with a huge black and white dog that was wagging its tail.

"Uh... maybe a smaller one? Let's shoot for medium or small in size, okay?"

"Okay," Dominic mumbled, dejected. "That wouldn't have been a problem at our old house."

As if realizing that he said something he shouldn't have, Dominic widened his eyes and looked guilty. I saw his gaze flicker over to Trainer. Crouching down beside him, I placed a hand on his back.

"You're right," I said in a low voice, so that Trainer couldn't hear us. "Our new home is smaller. But it'll be a loving one for the new dog, right?"

Dominic nodded. "Right."

And he continued on. It wasn't ideal that Dominic mentioned our old home in front of Trainer, but I knew that I'd eventually have to tell him the truth anyway. I would have to trust him with it when I felt that I was ready. I was too embarrassed to talk about it yet.

Dominic reached the end of the row of cages with Trainer and I trailing along behind. Suddenly, he got serious, as if he recognized the weight of his decision. Turning, he walked back along the row of cages, once again peering inside.

"This kid's an old soul, huh?" Trainer asked, and I nodded.

"He's always wanted a dog, but... we weren't allowed to have one at our old place." It wasn't technically a lie. "I'm sorry, it might take a while for him to pick one. It's a huge deal for him."

"I've got nowhere to be," Trainer said as he stuck his fingers into a cage for an especially excited puppy to sniff.

I kept my eyes on Dominic. He was barely slowing down as he passed some cages, while he paused at others, looking thoughtful. I wasn't sure what he was looking for in a dog, but he seemed determined to find it.

In the meantime, I was concerned about the seventy-five dollar adoption fee. It was good that the dogs came vaccinated and spayed or neutered, but that was still a lot of money on my small salary. I still had to buy supplies too.

Finally, Dominic stopped walking, peering into a cage with a soft smile. "This is the one I want," announced confidently.

Coming up behind him, I looked in the cage and saw a small ball of brown fur curled up in the middle. He'd lifted his head and was looking at us curiously. One of his ears was mangled, and there were long scars on his muzzle.

"Why this one?" I asked, but I thought I might already know the answer.

"He's been hurt. Someone needs to take care of him," he looked up at me. "He belongs with us."

For a long moment, I couldn't speak around the lump in my throat.

"I'll go get the girl at the front desk," Trainer said. I barely registered his leaving.

"Dominic, are you sure about this? You don't have to

pick this dog just because he's been injured. Do you think he's like you?"

"No. He's like you, mom. But look," he nodded to the dog that was now standing, "he's okay now."

This kid gutted me without even realizing it.

"Have we picked a new furry friend?" the cheerful voice of the shelter employee let me know that I had to pull myself together. I couldn't go to pieces right now. I blinked several times to make sure there weren't tears in my eyes while I was still facing away from her and Trainer.

"Yes," Dominic answered. "I want this one."

"Are you sure about that?" she asked me with a slight frown. "That dog has some past trauma, I'm sure you can see that, but it means he might need some special care. Extra attention."

"What exactly happened to him?" I asked, knowing that it didn't matter if he was difficult. Dominic was right. He belonged with us.

"He was rescued from a dog-fighting ring along with three others. They all had to be put down."

"That's horrible."

"They were all so aggressive. We worked with them for weeks, but got nowhere. So we had no choice. This little guy was different because he was used as a bait dog."

My heart hurt. I could just imagine this small dog being chained up and attacked over and over just so that other innocent animals could get a taste for blood that would ultimately cause their deaths. There was a special place in hell for people that did these things.

"We'll take him. I'm sure."

"Okay. We'll have to go slow, don't want to freak him out. Here," she handed Dominic a couple of dog treats from her pocket.

Trainer and I stood back as she opened the cage. Dominic went down on his knees in front of the cage at her direction, holding out his hand with the dog treat and waiting. It seemed to take forever, and I was impressed by Dominic's patience. He didn't move a muscle, even when the dog started to creep forward. Its head was lowered and tail tucked between its legs.

Now that it was standing and coming closer, I could see that there was also scarring on its legs. It wasn't as obvious because the hair around the scars was thicker, helping to cover the damage. As the dog got closer to Dominic, the smile on his face got bigger.

Trainer reached out and took my hand as the dog finally got close enough to Dominic to extend his neck and reach the treat. Before taking it, he sniffed Dominic's hand, looking into his eyes. I could almost swear that I could see a connection forming between them. When the dog decided that he'd sniffed Dominic enough, it took the treat and even allowed itself to be petted. It did flinch for a second, but once Dominic scratched behind its ears, they both relaxed.

This was the forging of a relationship that was going to last for years, and I was so glad that I agreed to get him a dog. Dominic would be comforted by having one. As I squeezed Trainer's hand, I wondered if I had found what I needed in him as well. It certainly felt like it.

"Does he have a name?" I asked.

The shelter worker shook her head, "No, not that we're aware of."

"Gizmo," Dominic said. "His name is Gizmo."

"Okay, I'll start the paperwork and get you guys out of here in a jiffy."

It didn't take long to complete the process, and the three of us were walking out of the building twenty minutes later with Gizmo on a leash, and Dominic looking happier than I'd ever seen him before.

"Thanks for being here," I said to Trainer as we got into the car. "I know it's not exactly a typical date…"

"Hey, I had fun. Don't tell anyone, because I have a tough-guy image to maintain, but I'm a sucker for puppies."

"I don't think I saw a single puppy in there."

"All dogs are puppies at heart."

As if to prove Trainer's point, Gizmo let out a bark before raising up on his hind legs and licking Dominic's face. It looked like he was happy to be coming home.

THIRTEEN
TRAINER

I wasn't sure exactly when I'd decided to move forward with Erica. I just couldn't seem to help myself when I saw her unexpectedly. So, I decided to get out of my way and do this already.

When I ran into her at the mall, I was with Pin, meeting up with a contact that had connections to Las Balas. Ryder was serious about putting a stop to their peddling of meth here in La Playa. It had been an issue before, but he took what happened with Carlos personally. Yesterday, our Prospects had been tasked with moving his shit out of his apartment in the Outlaw Souls complex.

I was pissed about it, but not nearly as much as Hawk. He'd sponsored Carlos, and the man's betrayal reflected badly on him. That was the problem with drugs like meth. People got so hooked that they lost their damn minds. Crystal meth was even worse because of the crap that it was made out of. Not only that, the labs had a nasty tendency of exploding. It was bad news all around.

The person we met at the mall was an old flame of the

Sergeant at Arms for Las Balas. She was bitter as hell because the guy kept promising to leave his wife and never followed through. So, it was easy to get information about the club from her. Their pillow talk had proven to be rather detailed, and we now knew that the Vice President was the one cooking the drugs.

We just had to figure out where the man did the deed. In the meantime, I was eating Chinese food on Erica's couch while we watched her son play with his new dog. I had never spent much time around kids, other than the younger ones that I met in the foster system, but I hadn't formed a connection with any of them. I was still getting to know Dominic, but I liked the kid. He was very well-behaved, so much so that I had to wonder if it was normal. Weren't seven-year-olds supposed to whine and complain?

Erica must have hit the lottery with this one.

We had gone to the store after the animal shelter, buying dog food, a dog crate, and a half dozen toys. I'd insisted on paying, even when Erica tried to say no. I didn't dare ask how much money she made teaching yoga at the fitness center, but it couldn't be much, and I didn't like the idea of her struggling.

The sound of a toddler throwing a tantrum came through the wall from the other half of the duplex.

"Yeah, the walls here are thin," Erica said with an annoyed frown.

"You hear that a lot?"

"Not always the same thing. Sometimes it's the parents fighting. The most annoying thing is when they're loud late at night. I've heard music playing after midnight before."

"What does the landlord have to say about it?"

"I haven't told him."

"Why not?"

"I just don't want to make trouble. I don't need the attention."

I studied her, trying to figure out what that meant, but she avoided my eyes. It was always a dead end with her.

"I'm going to clean up," she said, gathering our take out containers and taking them into the kitchen. I decided to follow her with Dominic's discarded food container, wanting to help out as well as steal a minute alone with her in the other room.

When I walked in, her back was to me as she filled up a glass with water at the sink. I paused, taking in the retro-styled kitchen and marveling that someone purposefully designed this space with so much wood paneling. Walking to the trash can in the corner, I threw out the empty cardboard container. I was approaching Erica when she turned around. She must not have heard me enter the kitchen because the sight of me startled her so much that she jumped, and the glass in her hand slipped out onto the floor where it shattered at her feet. She was only wearing socks.

"Don't move," I barked, hurrying forward to get her away from the glass before she hurt herself.

To my horror, she flinched and backed up. There was stark terror on her face that made me freeze, despite the urge to lift her off her feet for her safety. I raised my hands up in front of me, palms up, in an effort to show her that I meant no harm.

Erica blinked. Once. Twice. Her expression cleared, but I could see her visibly shaking.

"I'm sorry," she said, her voice breaking. She started to take a step forward, but stopped, letting out a whimper of pain. I looked down and saw that there was blood on the floor under her right foot.

"Damn it," I grumbled. Careful not to move too quickly

since she still looked a little jumpy, I closed the space between us. "It's okay. I'm not going to hurt you."

"I know that," she responded immediately, sounding like she meant it. "I don't... it's not you."

That was good to know, but I was going to need the whole story sooner rather than later. The pieces were starting to come together, and I didn't like what I was seeing.

My boots crunching the glass pieces into powder as I wrapped my arms around Erica's waist and lifted her into the air. I perched her on the edge of the countertop and stepped back.

"Give me your foot."

Erica looked fragile and embarrassed as she lifted her foot straight out for me. I took a hold of her ankle and bent down to see the damage. It was hard to tell with her sock on and all the blood, but it looked like she had a piece of glass stuck in her heel.

"Is it bad?" she asked.

"I can't tell for sure yet, but I don't think so. It's just a good thing I'm not squeamish."

I glanced up at her face, and she offered a weak smile.

"I think I'm going to have to cut your sock off to see it better."

Erica reached over and grabbed a pair of scissors off the knife block next to her. I got to work cutting along the sides of her sock, making sure to avoid her skin.

It was funny, I'd stitched up myself and other Outlaw Souls in the past after knife wounds, but I'd never felt this nervous about it. Erica was delicate, and she needed a gentle touch. Too bad, she was stuck with mine instead.

But I was going to do my best to help her.

"Mom?" Dominic's voice was in the doorway of the

kitchen, giving me no time to stop him from coming in and seeing the bloody mess.

"It's okay, buddy. I'm alright."

I turned to see Dominic with Gizmo at his side on the other end of the room. He didn't look terrified like I expected. Instead, he almost looked angry.

"Did he hurt you?" he asked Erica as if I wasn't standing right there.

"No. It was just an accident. I promise."

Was it weird that he jumped to that conclusion? I wasn't sure, but it sure as hell didn't feel good to have him accusing me of something like that.

"Make sure you keep the dog back and don't come any closer yourself," I told him, trying to show that I wasn't the bad guy here. "There's still broken glass over here."

"Why don't you take the dog out into the backyard to use the bathroom?" Erica suggested.

Dominic did as she asked just as I pulled the sock from her foot. It looked like I was right. A single piece of glass was stuck in her heel, but it didn't look too deep. I was no expert, but I'd say that it would be fine without needing stitches.

"Do you have a first aid kit around here somewhere?"

"Under the kitchen sink."

I got it out and opened it on the counter, digging through until I found a tube of antibiotic ointment and a bandage.

"You want some pain killer?" I asked, holding up a bottle of Tylenol.

Erica held out her hand. "Yeah, it'll have to do for now. I have edibles, but I won't eat them until Dominic is in bed for the night."

I handed over the bottle, and she shook out three into

the palm of her hand. Before I could get her a glass of water, she took them dry.

"Alright, I'm going to pull out the glass now," I said, picking up a dish towel to grab the sharp edge with. "It's going to hurt."

Erica nodded, and I saw that fighter's strength on her face that I had noticed when we first met. She may have had a moment of weakness before, but she was still a warrior.

"Ready? One... two... three."

Erica yipped in pain as I pulled out the glass, dropping it on the floor and pressing the towel to her wound to stop the bleeding.

"Here, hold that in place. I want to get the glass cleaned up before Dominic comes back in."

"*You're* going to clean it up?" she asked, looking startled.

"Well, yeah. If you tell me where the broom is."

"The pantry."

She bent her knee to bring her foot closer and held the towel against it. I peeked out the window and saw that Dominic was playing fetch with the dog in the fenced-in yard. It looked like we would be alone for a while.

I grabbed the broom, but leaned it against the wall. Coming close to Erica, I took her face in both of my hands, kissing her lips. I leaned my forehead against hers.

"Can you tell me what's going on?" I asked. It was a simple question, but absolutely vital.

"I think I have to, don't I?"

"No," I said firmly with a shake of my head. "But I don't see how we can have a real relationship if I don't know what you're hiding."

Erica took a deep, shuddering breath. "Fair enough. You sweep, and I'll talk, okay?"

That sounded like a good deal to me, so I picked up the broom and got to work. It was finally time to hear Erica's story.

FOURTEEN
ERICA

I had never told the truth to anyone. For a long time, I believed there was no one to tell. I had no friends, no family. I was afraid to report it to the police. What if they didn't believe me? Jeff would have been furious, and I wouldn't have a way to escape his wrath.

Now, it was finally time to unload this burden. I trusted Trainer. Some people might think it was too soon, but I had to follow my gut when it came to him. Watching him work his way around the kitchen, sweeping up a mess that would have gotten me a thorough beating in the past, I felt safe.

"My name is not Erica Mills," I started. Trainer stopped sweeping and looked at me. I wasn't sure what he expected, but it definitely wasn't that.

"It's a fake name that I took on when I moved here. My real name is Eve Donovan."

Trainer looked out the window into the backyard once again. "And Dominic?"

"I thought it would be too difficult for him to adapt to a new first name at his age. He has enough to remember with a new surname and backstory."

Trainer nodded and went back to sweeping, which I took as a sign to continue.

"I told you my parents died when I was eighteen. Well, I guess my story begins right after that. I was about to go to college to pursue a degree in business, but I didn't take the death of my parents well. My life basically fell apart."

It was a dark time for me, the period of my life up to that point. I didn't like to think about it because it always led to dwelling on what could have been.

"I was sad and lost, trying to figure out how to come to terms with my parents' deaths and move on with my life. It was during this time that I met Jeff."

Trainer stiffened, but didn't speak, so I continued. "He seemed, great at first, a dream come true. He gave me the attention that I needed and brought an end to my loneliness. He was rich and charming. I thought I was in love. So, we got married just days after my nineteenth birthday. Jeff said he wanted to take care of me. He built us a perfect house in a perfect neighborhood. All I had to do was be the perfect housewife," my voice was dripping with bitterness.

Trainer had finished sweeping up the glass and dumped it into the trash. Now, he was leaning against the refrigerator, watching me silently. I was glad that he wasn't interrupting. This was hard enough already.

"I got pregnant with Dominic quickly. We'd only been married a few months. Jeff had become overbearing after our wedding, taking control of every aspect of my life, but he didn't lay a hand on me until after our son was born."

Trainer's jaw clenched, and I knew he wasn't going to like this next part.

"He started beating on me just after Dominic's birth. I remember the first time," my voice was soft as the memory replayed in my mind. "We'd gone out to dinner with some of his coworkers and their wives. He's a big-time businessman, you see, and I had gotten caught up in a conversation with one of the men. I don't remember what we talked about... music, I think. It doesn't matter. What's important is that Jeff thought that I was flirting with the guy right in front of him. He waited until we were home, and the babysitter had left before he started calling me a whore. I used to argue back in the beginning, so it escalated quickly. He slapped me across the face.

"It shocked me more than it hurt, and I immediately started threatening to leave him. But he apologized, begged me to stay, promised it would never happen again. So I stayed."

I shook my head at my stupidity. "You know, I want to say that was the only time I fell for those lies, but it wasn't. I think I wanted to believe it, even though I knew damn well that it wasn't true. It just kept happening, over any perceived infraction. I swear, he *looked* for reasons."

"Bastard," Trainer growled, and for some reason, I found his simmering anger comforting. It made me feel like I wasn't alone in this horror story.

"Yeah," I agreed. "He is. And I eventually realized that. The times that he was loving became fewer and fewer until I felt like I was living in constant fear. Dominic was a toddler at the time and starting to get an idea of what was going on."

"What about Dominic? Did he-"

"No. He never hit him, thank God."

Trainer crossed his arms over his chest, not looking relieved in the slightest. I twisted my fingers together in my lap. Why was this so hard to talk about?

"But no one knew what was going on?"

"No. Jeff is smart. He kept me isolated from people, as much as possible, to keep me dependent on him. And after that first time, when he left me with a swollen face and busted lip, he got more careful, only leaving marks in places that could be easily covered with clothing."

Trainer opened his mouth to speak, but seemed to rethink his words as his lips snapped closed once again.

"What do you want to say?" I asked.

"I don't want to make it seem like I'm judging you... I just, I don't understand why you stayed. Why didn't you report him to the police?"

"I wanted to leave many times. But Jeff had me convinced that he had the power to stop me. The man likes to throw around money, and he always told me that he knew cops that he could pay off to make me look like a liar or a crazy person. Then, I would be at his mercy. And he promised me that I would lose Dominic if I left him. He can afford the best lawyers, and I couldn't take that risk. He never hit Dominic, but what would he do to him when I wasn't around?"

"People like that need to have someone at their mercy," Trainer said. His voice was cold, but it didn't scare me. "It's the only way they can feel good about themselves by pushing around others."

"So, I saved up as much money as I could, and I ran. We can't let him find us. He has such a temper. Honestly, I think that if Jeff got his hands on me again, he might lose it and kill me."

"Like hell, he will."

"I just wish I was strong enough to stop him from hurting me, to protect Dominic from the things he's seen. If I wasn't so damn weak..." I bit my lip.

Trainer was in front of me in the blink of an eye. Placing his large hands on my shoulders, he looked into my eyes, his brown orbs burning into mine.

"I don't want to hear you talk like that ever again. I've seen your strength since the moment we met, shining through your eyes. Just because some pencil-dick asshole took advantage of his physical strength over you, doesn't make you weak. Look at that little boy out there, running around like he doesn't have a care in the world. You did that for him. It can't have been easy to leave behind everything you knew and go into hiding from a fucking monster."

No, it wasn't. I wanted to believe Trainer's words because I could see that they were sincere, but I'd spent so long feeling ashamed of myself that it was hard to let go of that feeling. Still. My heart warmed, knowing that he saw me as strong.

"You know, my real hair color is red," I said. I wanted him to know the real me as much as possible. I had been trying to embrace this new persona, but I couldn't help feeling like an imposter every day.

"I wondered about that. Your reaction to that picture I saw on your phone makes a lot more sense now."

"Yeah," I grimaced. "I haven't been great at hiding my secrets, have I?"

"Well, I had my suspicions, but I'm glad you finally trusted me enough to tell me the truth."

"And you still want to stick around?"

"Why wouldn't I?"

"It's a lot to take in, isn't it? There's a looming threat in the picture. Lots of people wouldn't want to get wrapped up in that."

"Any man that would walk away from a woman he cares

about instead of protecting her is a piece of shit that doesn't deserve her in the first place."

"How poetic," I teased.

"I never claimed to be good with words," he shrugged. "Now, let's look at that foot."

I looked down, seeing that the bleeding had stopped. I'd been so wrapped up in my story that I'd nearly forgotten about it. Now that I was thinking about the wound, I started to notice the throbbing pain. I'd been stupid to freak out like that when I dropped the glass. Trainer wasn't Jeff. I was sure that he'd never hurt me.

That belief was solidified as he took my foot into his hand. Using a wet washcloth, he cleaned the blood off the bottom of my foot, taking his time and being extra gentle around the wound. It still stung a little, but I suppressed any reaction. Trainer slathered the bandage in antibiotic ointment and covered the cut. He helped me off the counter just as Dominic came in the backdoor.

"You okay, mom?" he asked, eyeing the blood that remained on the floor.

"Yep," I said brightly. It was true. My foot was sore, but it would heal. It was the sharing of my story with Trainer that had had the biggest impact on me. I felt like a weight had been lifted off of my chest, and I could breathe easier. "I just have to mop up this mess, and we'll be good."

"No way," Trainer said. "I'll do that. Why don't you and Dominic go pick out a movie to watch?"

"Are you sure?"

"Hundred percent. Now, go."

Dominic and I picked out an animated feature, putting it into the DVD-player and cuddling up on the couch until Trainer joined us.

By the time we got through the opening credits, my eyelids were heavy. Trainer's arm went around my shoulders, and I rested my cheek on his chest. Relaxing, I let my eyes flutter closed, as the steady beat of Trainer's heart lulled me to sleep.

FIFTEEN
TRAINER

I was harboring a murderous rage. Where was a punching bag when you needed one?

Not that I would trade my current location for anything else. Sitting on the couch with Erica nestled into my side, I felt her curvy body relax into mine, and her deep breathing told me that she'd fallen asleep. I glanced over at Dominic and saw that he was still awake, watching this cartoon movie that Erica had put in, but he was blinking slowly, and his head was dropping. I figured he'd be out like a light soon enough.

That meant my mind was free to roam, and there was only one subject that I could focus on right now. That fucking husband of hers.

I wanted to teach him a lesson that he'd never forget. It had taken all my willpower not to curse and rage against the man while I was in the kitchen with Erica, but I could see that it was taking a lot out of her to share already. The last thing I wanted was to make her regret it.

What kind of a man does this to a woman?

I didn't have any answers.

All I knew for sure was that I didn't want to be away from her right now. So, I waited until Dominic had fallen asleep. When he was out for the night, I rearranged Erica so that I could get off the couch without disturbing her. Scooping Dominic up, I took him up the stairs to his room. Gizmo was curled up on his new pet bed on the floor, and he lifted his head as we passed, watching his boy. He stayed in place, though.

Dominic didn't wake up at all, even when I put him on the bed, pulling off his white tennis shoes. I felt a curious affection for the boy as I covered his body with his blanket, and he shifted in the bed, letting out a contented sigh in his sleep. Up until today, I'd been viewing Dominic almost as an obstacle on the path to Erica. He was important to her, so I *had* to get to know him.

It turned out that I liked him. He was a good kid that had been dealt a bad hand in life up until now. I could relate to that.

I turned on a nightlight in the wall socket before I slipped out of the room. When I got back downstairs, Erica was curled up on her side on the couch, looking so small that all I wanted to do was protect her. I turned off the TV and was struck by how normal this domestic stuff felt. I'd never considered myself a traditional man, certainly not the type to hang out with a kid, but I was comfortable here.

I knelt next to the couch and gathered Erica into my arms. Lifting her up, I started toward the stairs. Erica's eyes opened slowly, and when she saw me, she gave me a sleepy smile.

"Where's Dominic?" she asked. Craning her next around, trying to catch sight of him.

"Sleeping in his room." I had started to climb the stairs, so I kept my voice quiet to avoid waking him.

Erica relaxed back into my body, closing her eyes once again. The way that she trusted me meant the world to me now that I knew the details of her past.

Erica's room was dark, but the hall light allowed me to see well enough to find her bed. Shifting her carefully in my arms, I managed to get the sheet and comforter pulled back before lowering her onto the mattress. She turned onto her side once again, snuggling into her pillow and letting out a sigh that was so much like Dominic's it made me want to laugh.

Just as I was turning away from the bed to leave, a small hand shot out and grabbed my wrist. "Don't go," Erica said, her voice sounding more awake than I expected. "Stay with me tonight. Please."

She didn't have to ask me twice. I pulled my shirt over my head and kicked off my boots. I thought about leaving my jeans on for her, but I didn't think I'd be able to sleep that way. So, they joined my boots on the floor and I slipped into the bed beside her wearing only my boxers.

Erica was facing away from me, so I moved closer until my chest was pressed against her back. My arm went around her waist, and her ass lined up just right with my cock. I could feel myself hardening, but I wasn't going to do anything about it. Not tonight. After Erica's story, I felt like both of our emotions were too raw to handle anything more physical than this. And for the first time, I wanted a woman to know that I was good for more than just sex. I could give her more.

"Goodnight, Trainer," she whispered in the darkness.

"Goodnight, Eve," I said, using her real name for the first time. I understood that I couldn't call her that, not if she wanted to maintain her fake identity. But just this once, while it was just the two of us in this space, I wanted to acknowledge the person she really was, the life that Jeff had effectively stolen from her.

She stiffened for a second but relaxed quickly. It was a matter of minutes before she was asleep again. I forced all thoughts of hunting down her ex-husband to teach him a lesson out of my mind and followed suit.

THE BONNEVILLE WAS COMING ALONG NICELY. It was amazing what a few simple changes, like a new seat and tires, could do for a bike like this. I'd given the thing a full service and taken it out for a test ride at the end of last week. It was a smooth ride for the most part. The only issue I noticed was when I tried to downshift. The gear lever would move as if going to a lower gear, but it wouldn't actually do it.

It was a simple enough fix, just requiring a new return spring, but I hadn't gotten the part in until today. So, I was at the shop, swapping out the defective spring for a new one. I anticipated having this bike up for sale by the end of the day.

My phone rang, and I hurriedly wiped my greasy hands clean before digging it out of my pocket. Mama Tammy was calling, and I managed to answer after three rings.

"Hello?" My voice was tense. She had to be calling with news about the biopsy.

"Hello, Raul. How are you?"

I bit back a demand that she tell me her news as soon as possible.

"I'm fine. Working on your future bike right now."

She let out an undignified sound that was half-grunt, half-chuckle. "Yeah, right."

"What about you, Mama? Are you okay?"

"I am," she said, and I could hear the smile in her voice. "I got a call from the doctor today. He said it's not cancer. Just a cyst or something like that."

"So... it's nothing to worry about?"

"That's right."

I felt like I could finally breathe easily for the first time since she told me about the biopsy.

"Thank God." I wasn't a religious man, but I meant those words. If he was out there, then I appreciated the hell out of this miracle.

"I know you're coming over in a few days, but I thought you'd want to know now."

"I did. Thank you." Her mention of our Sunday visit made something occur to me. "Hey, do you think it would be okay if I brought someone when I come to visit you on Sunday? Well, two people."

"You know anyone is welcome. Two people? Are they friends of yours?"

"It's a woman I'm seeing and her son."

There was a beat of silence. Then, "Lordy, I had no idea you were even seeing a woman. How long has this been going on? What's her name? You say she has a son? How old is the boy?"

"Whoa, slow down," I said, but her enthusiasm made me smile. "Her name is Erica, and yes, she has a seven-year-old son named Dominic."

"Seven, huh? I can work with that."

"What's that mean?"

"You know I fostered for many years. I still have tons of toys and games in storage. I'll find some things for him to play with."

"I still have to ask if she wants to come."

"Don't be silly. Of course, she will. If not, you'll convince her. You can be very charming, you know."

"I'm not so sure about that," I said. "But I'll do my best."

"Well, I need to go. I have so much cleaning to do before Sunday."

I rolled my eyes. "You don't need to do anything special. I'm not bringing the damn Queen. Erica is very down-to-earth."

"Language," she admonished, but she sounded distracted. "I'll talk to you later, Raul. I just saw a cobweb in the corner. The house needs to be dusted."

The line went dead, and I tucked my phone back into my pocket, still grinning.

SIXTEEN

ERICA

I ran my hands over my skirt, smoothing it down. Then, I opened the visor above my head to check that my hair wasn't frizzy. I was meeting Trainer's foster mother, and there were butterflies in my stomach. This felt like a big step, and I wanted it to go well. I kept wanting to chew on my fingernails - a bad habit that I'd had since I was a child - but I was forcing myself not to do it. I didn't want my fingernail polish to chip.

We were in Trainer's truck, a red crew-cab. It was weird seeing him in a vehicle like this. The man seemed to be made for riding. He looked so natural there. But the truck was nice, with heated leather seats and a quiet engine. It was also meticulously clean, making me think that he didn't drive it much.

When we pulled up in front of his foster mother's house, Trainer put the car in park and reached over to grab my hand, which was brushing imaginary lint off my blouse.

"Don't worry," he said, giving my fingers a squeeze.

"I'm not worried," I lied.

"Oh, so this level of fidgeting is normal for you?"

"Maybe," I replied stubbornly.

"Okay, then. My bad," Trainer said, releasing my hand and opening his car door. "I'm glad you're not nervous, because she's excited to meet you."

His eyes were fixed on the porch, and I followed his gaze. There was a plump, black woman waving in our direction. She was wearing a floral print dress and had a white dish towel thrown over her shoulder.

Trainer helped Dominic out of his booster seat while I stepped from the truck. I liked that he did that. Instead of hurrying around to open my car door, he prioritized Dominic, which earned him far more points in my book.

Dominic wasn't nervous at all. He'd come out of his shell so much in the last few weeks that he liked meeting new people now. I wasn't even sure why I was anxious.

When we reached the porch, Trainer's foster mother pulled him into a hug. "Raul, you look so handsome today," she cooed. He'd pulled his long hair into a ponytail at the back of his neck and trimmed his beard. I had to agree with her. He looked good.

"Thanks, Mama. This is Erica," he said, pulling away from her. "Erica, this is my foster mother, Tammy Whitford."

I stepped forward with my hand extended. "Nice to meet-"

My words were cut off when she engulfed me in a hug as well, squeezing until I could hardly breathe.

"I'm thrilled that Raul has finally brought home a woman. And you're lovely," she stepped back, but kept ahold of my arms as she looked me up and down. "So pretty."

"Oh, uh, thanks, Mrs. Whitford."

"No, no, no. It's Mama Tammy or just Mama if you'd

like. After fostering children for twenty years, I don't know how to respond to anything else. Now, this must be your boy."

Dominic had been lingering just behind me, and when Tammy spotted him, she flashed a warm smile in his direction.

"Yes, this is Dominic."

The four of us headed into the house. I realized how hungry I was when I saw a pan of sliced roast beef on the counter, still steaming as if it had just been pulled from the oven. There was also a pan of buttered potatoes and one of glazed carrots. Talk about comfort food.

"Can I help you with anything?" I asked.

"Aren't you a doll?" Tammy smiled. "I'm all done in here. Just a matter of grabbing plates and loading up. Please, don't be shy. I don't need leftovers."

"That's true. She usually sends them home with me," Trainer said.

"Well, I have to know that you have *some* good food." She leaned closer to me and spoke in a stage whisper, "He's hopeless in the kitchen."

"I heard that," Trainer grumbled.

We all grabbed a plate off the counter and started loading them up. It was a little chaotic, especially with Trainer's large presence in the small kitchen, but we all managed to get what we wanted and take a seat at the kitchen table.

"Your home is really nice, so clean," I said once we were all seated.

"Thank you," Tammy replied, shooting Trainer a smug look that I didn't understand.

As we ate together, Tammy shared stories about Trainer, some that made him groan and roll his eyes. Like the time he locked himself out of the house in his underwear when he was seventeen.

"I'd made him take his shoes off outside the day before because he had gotten them muddy at football practice," Tammy began.

"Football?" I asked, raising an eyebrow.

"Yeah, I gave it a shot. I was the biggest kid in my class, so it seemed like a good idea. The problem was that I don't actually like the game."

"Bit of an oversight on your part," I said drily.

"Anyway," Tammy continued. "I was already at work when he stepped outside to grab the shoes. Of course, he wasn't dressed yet, just wearing a pair of boxers, and when he closed the door behind himself, it was locked."

I giggled at the image in my mind.

"I'm happy you guys find this so amusing," Trainer said, letting out a long-suffering sigh.

Tammy kept talking as if he hadn't spoken, "The worst part was that he not only missed the school bus, but was outside, trying to climb up onto the roof when it drove by. They all got quite a show."

"No," Trainer said, "the worst part was when I decided to try the back door and had to scale the privacy fence. Not easy even when you're fully clothed. The glorious end of the adventure was when I landed in Mama Tammy's rosebush on the other side."

"Ouch," I winced. Dominic laughed.

"Okay, very funny," Trainer said. "Let's move on to something else."

"How about the time you almost burned the house down, making grilled cheese?" Tammy suggested with a wide grin.

We all laughed, except for Trainer, but he did look

amused. Looking between Tammy and Trainer, I could see the love there. They might not be related by blood, but they were family. A small part of me was jealous, having lost that when my parents died so many years ago. But I didn't resent Trainer for it. More than anything, I was happy to be here. I hoped that Dominic visited me this often when he was a grown man.

After dinner concluded, Tammy and I cleared the table, sending Trainer and Dominic into the other room to poke around in Tammy's toy closet, trying to find something that might keep Dominic entertained.

I offered to clean the dishes since Tammy had done all the work of making us a delicious meal, but she wouldn't have it. Instead, I washed while she dried and put the dishes away. She did pack up the leftovers in Tupperware containers for Trainer to take.

Dominic's laughter floated in from the other room, my favorite sound in the world. I didn't know what he and Trainer were up to, but it sounded like they were having fun. Who knew that Trainer was just a big kid at heart?

"He's a very polite young man," Tammy commented as she ran her towel over a plate and added it to a stack that was ready to be put away.

"Yeah, I don't know how I got so lucky as to have such a good kid."

"You ever think about having more?"

Her words were carefully innocent, but I was no fool. Pulling my hands out of the sink, I dripped water onto the floor but hardly noticed.

"Look, Tammy," she gave me a stern look, so I corrected myself. "*Mama Tammy*, Trainer and I haven't been seeing each other for very long. I mean, we haven't even..."

Nope, not going to tell her that we haven't slept together yet.

"We're still getting to know each other," I finished.

"Oh, I know," she said dismissively. "But I've never seen Trainer like this. He's never brought a woman here, never even talked about a woman he was seeing. I've known that boy for nearly eighteen years, and you are the very first. You're special. I promise I'm not picking out China patterns, but I am curious about what you want out of this relationship. Or what you have planned for your future."

My stomach felt like it was knotted into a fist. I was still married to Jeff, and I wasn't sure that would ever change. To divorce him, I'd have to tell him where I am. The idea of him locating me was terrifying.

Did I see a future with Trainer? Maybe. But I didn't think I had the luxury of a normal life anymore. Jeff's existence was like a guillotine hanging over my head. More kids would mean more danger. Really committing would mean that if Jeff found me, it would be that much harder to leave.

That was my ultimate move, my last resort to keep us safe. I couldn't give that up, no matter how much I cared for Trainer.

TAMMY and I were once again in the locker room together. I had been thinking a lot lately about my life here in La Playa, and I wanted to stay if I could. That would mean setting up a fake identity for myself and Dominic. I needed to be able to open a checking account, get health insurance, and have a driver's license if I got pulled over. I had to officially embrace my new identity with a paper trail. The problem was that I had no idea where to get such a thing.

"Hey, Tammy, can I ask you a question?"

"Shoot," she said distractedly as she pulled on a pair of jeans.

"Before I do, it's really important that you keep this between us."

Tammy stopped rifling through her gym bag and took a seat on the bench beside me.

"Okay. Mum's the word. What do you need?"

"A fake ID."

Tammy looked confused. "That's it? You had me worried there for a second."

"Yes, but it needs to be really good. Do you know where I can get one?"

"Right across the street."

"At the bar?"

"Yep. You want an Outlaw Soul named Hawk. His work is impeccable."

"Perfect," I said, pulling my shirt over my head and closing my locker. I could head over there real quick before picking up Dominic. "Thanks, Tammy."

"Wait, Erica. Are you okay?"

"Yeah," I smiled. "I will be."

As soon as I made this identity official, I hoped I'd be fine.

I drove across the street and parked at The Blue Dog. I automatically scanned the parking lot for Trainer's bike, but he wasn't here. I probably should have asked him where to get a fake ID, but I didn't want to admit that I might have to leave someday if this didn't work out. I was afraid it would burst the bubble of happiness that had formed around us. Right now, I needed that happiness.

Walking into the bar was different this time. There weren't nearly as many people here on a weeknight, and when I entered, it felt like all eyes were on me. It occurred to me that I didn't know anyone in the Outlaw Souls other than Trainer and Swole. I recognized the patch on many of the patron's jackets, but I had no idea which one was Hawk, if he was even here.

Approaching the bar, I didn't bother taking a seat. The bartender was different from the one that had been working the night I was here. This was a thin, young man with jet black hair and a diamond stud in one ear. He gave me the impression of someone that was trying very carefully to look tough but not quite pulling it off. Not everyone could be Swole. It took a moment for him to notice me standing there since he was filling four glasses with whatever beer they had on draft and flirting with the waitress.

When I finally caught his eye, he came right over. "What can I get ya?"

"I'm looking for a man named Hawk," I said, assuming that the bartender would know who that was since this was an Outlaw Souls hangout.

"You've come to the right place then," he said, gesturing to a table in the corner where two bikers were sitting by the window. They were under a neon light that cast them in a red glow. It looked almost ominous. I walked over, stopping just a few feet away.

"I'm looking for Hawk," I said.

"You found him," the man with the goatee said, looking at me curiously.

"Can we speak alone?" I asked. This needed to be done with as few as possible people finding out.

"Beat it," the man with the goatee said to the other. He did as he was told, getting up and walking over to claim a barstool.

"You're Hawk?" I asked, making sure before I took a seat.

"The one and only." He used his booted foot to push out a chair opposite his seat. I took it and sat down. "What can I do for you?"

"I hear that you are the man to see about a fake ID."

"Some might say that," he said non-committedly, he didn't look particularly interested in helping me out. "Why don't you tell me who flapped their jaw to you?"

I assumed that he was being careful and not looking to give anyone a hard time. At least, that's what I hoped. I'd hate to get Tammy into trouble. "Tammy Holt."

The suspicion cleared from his eyes, and he looked more alert. "Okay, what have you got for me?"

"I need two fake identities. One for me, and one for my son."

Hawk looked at me with a piercing gaze for almost a full minute. I couldn't resist squirming under his scrutiny. "You and your son? That's interesting. Let me tell you what I can do for you. I can make two kinds of fake IDs. Good or great. A good one will fool a bartender or store clerk. Basically, you're using someone's information - name, address, and all - and just putting your picture with it. It's what I usually make for teenagers that want to bar hop. It works, and it's affordable.

"But a great one is more than just an ID. It's a whole profile. Name, social security number, birthday, all of that shit. It's building a new life that will pass scrutiny. You can get a driver's license and passport. I'm guessing that's what you're looking for. Am I right?"

"Yes," I said, a little shaken by how quickly he deduced that.

"It won't be cheap. And I'll need the money upfront."

I gulped. I was worried about that. "How much?"

"For two? Hmm," he looked thoughtful. "I can do it for twenty-five hundred."

My heart sank. Over two thousand dollars? I didn't have that kind of money. I'd already gone through all the money that I'd taken from Jeff when I left him, and I was now firmly in the living paycheck-to-paycheck category.

"Okay," I said, because I really didn't have a choice. I needed this. "I can try to get the money to you tomorrow. Will you be here?"

"Most likely. If I'm not, one of the boys here will know how to find me."

I had brought one valuable thing with me to La Playa. It had been tucked away in my sock drawer since the day we arrived. It looked like it was time to get it out and see exactly what I could get for it. I wouldn't have a rainy day fund to fall back on, but we'd be able to stay and build lives here. It would be worth it.

SEVENTEEN
TRAINER

"I have news," Swole said as soon as I answered my phone. Straight to the point without even a greeting. That was typical Swole.

"What is it?"

"The drug dealer you spotted at the boardwalk finally led us somewhere."

I stood up from my couch, ready for whatever was needed of me. I tucked my gun into my pants at the small of my back and reached for my jacket.

"What's the plan? Did you find where the bastard is cooking his shit?"

"We did. And that's why I called you. We need to move Erica for a day or two."

"What?" Her words didn't make sense to me. "What did you say about Erica?"

"It's the location. The Sergeant at Arms of Las Balas has been cooking at his baby mama's house, in the basement. It's the other half of Erica's duplex."

My stomach rolled. Erica had been living right next to that dangerous shit for weeks. With Dominic. *Fuck.*

"Are you sure?"

"Yes," Swole said, sounding impatient. "We already went in and found the lab. Moves knows a guy that had experience cleaning this shit up, and he says it'll be safe, but I figured you'd want Erica out there just in case the whole thing blows up or something."

I felt a new kind of fear at those words. That could have happened already. How many times had I seen that sort of thing on the news? Too many.

I needed her with me right now. Dominic too.

"Where is she?"

"I gave her your address. I'm going to watch the dog for her since my apartment is on the ground floor. Emory has been wanting one anyway. So it'll be a good test to see how he handles it. Anyway, Erica seemed pretty damn reluctant to just show up on your doorstep, but I told her I'd already talked to you, and you insisted."

"Good call." There was a soft knock at my door. "She's here. Thanks for the head's up and for keeping her safe."

"Of course." Swole hung up, and I glanced around the apartment. It was a mess, but there wasn't much I could do about that. She was already here. There was another knock. It looked like she was going to get a glimpse of what a slob I could be. But, to be fair, I was a bachelor.

"Just a second," I called out to her.

Removing my gun, I quickly put it in the small safe in the linen closet between the bedroom and living room. I crossed the room and pulled the door open. Erica was standing there, chewing on her bottom lip with Dominic at her side. She looked stressed out, and I wanted to make it better.

"Hey," she said in a small voice.

"Come on in."

They both stepped inside, and I shut the door, locking it. It was a safe building, being owned by the Outlaw Souls, but since we all lived in the same place, privacy could be an issue. It wasn't unusual for someone to pop in just to see what I was up to. I hurried across the living room to the couch and grabbed the dirty clothes that I had haphazardly discarded there. There was also an empty pizza box on the coffee table that I managed to get to the trash can as well.

"Have a seat," I said.

Dominic sat on the couch, but Erica stayed standing. "Listen, this is really nice of you, but I don't want to put you out. We can stay in a hotel for a couple of days."

"No. I want you here. I want to know you're safe."

"A hotel would be safe."

"Being with me would be safer."

I meant it. Nothing would happen to either of them if they were with me, but I *did* wish that I had a slightly bigger apartment. My one-bedroom set-up was a little problematic. But I would make it work. It would be nice to share a bed with Erica again. We hadn't spent the night together since the day she told me about her husband. I got the impression that she didn't want to make overnights a regular thing right away for Dominic's sake.

"You're a good man, Trainer."

I wondered if she'd say that if she knew the things I was fantasizing about doing to her body. I was far from selfless. Then there was the fact that I wanted to beat her husband, visiting the pain he'd caused her back on his head and then some. I wanted to avenge her *and* stake a claim.

No, I didn't think I was a good man, but I promised myself that I would always be good to her.

"Why don't you put your bag in the bedroom," I said,

nodding in that direction. "Ignore the mess. It's the maid's week off."

Erica giggled as she headed through the bedroom door. I turned to Dominic.

"You doing okay, buddy?"

"I guess. I didn't have the time to grab any toys or anything."

"Oh. Well, I might be able to help you with that."

Going over to the entertainment center, I opened it up, exposing my game systems.

"Wow! Look at all that," Dominic shot up off the couch and came to my side. "You have everything! Playstation, the Switch, Xbox... What's that one?"

He was pointing to the smallest system of the bunch. "That's the NES Classic. That's what my original old Nintendo looked like only it was bigger. The company released this version a few years back, and it has all kinds of games that I grew up playing on it."

"Can we play that?"

"Of course. It happens to be one of my favorites."

When Erica came out of the bedroom ten minutes later, looking delectable in a pair of pajama pants and a tank top - with no bra, I noticed - we were both seated side-by-side on the living room floor, trying to pick a game from the wide selection.

"I've always been fond of Donkey Kong," Erica said, taking a seat on the couch behind us. I looked back at her as she smiled warmly at the two of us together. Our eyes met, and she mouthed, "thank you."

"Let's play Donkey Kong," Dominic agreed.

So, that's what we did for the next hour. I hadn't played this game in years, and Dominic was a fast learner, so he ended up being much better than me. He found that hilarious.

Finally, it was nine o'clock, and Erica announced that it was Dominic's bedtime. Since the only option for a bed for him was the couch, Erica and I had to go into the bedroom. I headed in there while she made the couch into a bed with my spare blankets. While in the bedroom, I picked up more dirty clothes, shoving them into the nearly full hamper.

I really needed to do some laundry.

And be more prepared for unexpected company.

I straightened out the blankets on the bed, but didn't bother making it properly. We were about to lay down anyway. When I decided the room looked passable, I pulled my shirt over my head. Just as I tossed it onto the overspilling hamper, Erica came in.

Her eyes scanned my torso, and I'd never been so happy that I worked out regularly. She looked hungry, and if Dominic wasn't in the next room, I'd already have her under me, writhing.

"Thanks for being cool with his bedtime. I really try to stick to it as much as possible."

"It's fine, really."

"I feel like such an idiot, like I made the wrong decision for us yet *again*. Of all the places in La Playa that I could have rented..."

"You're not being fair to yourself. You couldn't have known what was going on in the other half of the duplex."

"Yeah, but I did know that the guy was creepy. He always gave me a bad feeling."

"But he never did anything to you, did he?" I'd kill him.

"No. Swole said he's a part of a rival club or something?"

I nodded. Crossing the room, I took her into my arms. "Las Balas. They're bad news. They do everything from human trafficking to this shit with the meth. Always avoid them if you can. I'm sorry that you somehow got caught up in all this."

Erica wrapped her arms around my waist, drawing me closer.

"I have to admit, this whole thing does have some fringe benefits," she said, trailing kisses across my chest. The light contact from her wet lips made every nerve ending in my body come to life.

"You're killing me, sweetheart," my voice was pleading, but I wasn't sure if I was begging her to stop or keep going.

She stopped. "Yeah, it's not a good idea with Dominic so nearby."

At least she looked just as disappointed as I was.

"Maybe we should go to bed," she suggested.

I could have used a nice, cold shower, but the sound of the running water would probably keep Dominic awake, so I shucked my jeans and got under the covers with her. My bed wasn't very big, so the two of us had no choice but to get close.

We laid facing each other in the darkness, our legs twisted together. I had one hand tucked beneath my pillow, and the other was resting on her hip. The streetlights shone through the part in the curtains, giving us just enough light to make out the outline of each other's faces.

"Can I ask you a question?" she asked after a few minutes of just laying there together.

"Anything."

"Have you ever killed anyone?"

I stilled, so surprised by her question that I didn't answer right away. I must have been quiet for too long because when she spoke again, her words came out as nervous babble.

"Nevermind. You don't have to answer. I'm such an idiot. I've probably offended you so much. I just have been wondering for so long and-"

"It's okay," I cut her off because I had a feeling she'd just keep rambling if I didn't. "But... what makes you ask that?"

"I don't know. I just thought... isn't that something that happens in motorcycle clubs?"

"Sometimes," I admitted. I wished the light was brighter so that I could make out her expression, to see if she was horrified by the stark truth. "But not always. Personally, no, I haven't. But I'm really no better than those that have. I've hurt people, Erica. I always have my reasons, but the fact is that I've been the bad guy in someone's story more than once. I just haven't crossed that line. But I would if I had to. To defend myself or my fellow club members, I would do it."

Erica didn't say anything in response, but she didn't pull away from me either.

"Is that a problem for you?"

"It should be, right? That's what I keep thinking. Wouldn't those words make most women hesitate, or even go running for the hills? But I don't want to do that. I won't pretend to understand everything about the Outlaw Souls. I don't think that's even possible if you're not a member, but I think I do understand you." Reaching, she laid the palm of her hand against my cheek, caressing it. "I think you're honorable."

I wasn't so sure about that, but it still made me feel like a man that was worthy of her. Waves of affection seemed to emanate from the center of my chest, warming me all the way to the tips of my fingers and toes.

We didn't say anything else after that. Even though it was early for me, I found myself so at peace and relaxed that I was starting to doze off just a few minutes later. The last thing I was aware of was Erica moving ever closer, until she was nuzzling my chest. Then, I was out.

THE NEXT MORNING, I woke up to the sound of cartoonish music. Lifting my head, I blinked away the sleep from my eyes and saw that my bedroom door was open. The music must have been coming from the tv.

The light coming in from around the curtains looked grey, so I couldn't tell what time it was. I glanced over to see that Erica was still asleep. Her hair was a tangled mess on her pillow, and I realized that she was snoring very lightly.

Adorable.

I turned to the nightstand and grabbed my phone. Unlocking it, I flinched at the bright light from the screen. It was just after eight in the morning. Knowing that Erica was a fan of sleeping in, I carefully disentangled our limbs and slipped out of the bed without shaking the bed too much. I pulled a pair of pajama pants that I rarely ever wore out of my bottom drawer and stepped into them.

When I came out into the living room, I found Dominic sitting on the floor in front of the couch, eating cereal, and watching cartoons. I didn't even know that I had a cartoon channel.

"Morning, kid," I said, making him jump and bump into his bowl. A little milk spilled onto the hardwood. He looked up at me, with panic clearly visible on his face.

Fuck Jeff Donovan.

"Don't worry about that," I told him, not moving a

muscle for a full minute. I learned my lesson with Erica. If she triggered a freakout, she just needed a moment to collect herself and remember that she was safe here. I assumed that Dominic would be the same.

Walking into the kitchen, I grabbed a rag and got it wet. I came back into the living room and knelt in front of him, wiping up the mess as he watched me with wide eyes.

"Listen carefully," I said, meeting his eyes so he could see how serious I was. "Accidents happen. I'm not mad about it. But even if I was, you don't *ever* need to fear me. Do you understand that?"

"Mom told you about my dad?"

"She did."

"I hate him."

"That's understandable," I sat on the floor beside him. "You saw some pretty bad stuff happen to your mom. It's only natural that you'd hate the person that caused it."

"You don't think that makes me bad too?"

"No. It just means that you love your mom. Nothing wrong with that."

Dominic smiled. "Are you going to stick around, Trainer?"

"I want to. Would you be okay with that?"

"Yeah. Just be nice to mom."

"Always." I climbed to my feet. "Now, I'm going to go get my own bowl of that cereal. Do you mind if I watch your show with you?"

"Okay," he agreed.

As I got myself a bowl, I also turned on the coffee pot. Erica had mentioned to me once that she couldn't start her day without a nice, big cup. I wanted her to be comfortable while staying with me. Maybe we could do this more often.

EIGHTEEN
ERICA

I parked my car in front of Better Pawn, a pawn shop right on the beach. Opening my purse, I pulled out the small black jewelry box. I didn't bother looking at what was inside. It didn't have any sentimental value to me anymore.

The pawnshop itself had metal bars on its dusty windows, and the sign overhead was missing a letter. As I stepped inside, it took a moment for my eyes to adjust to the darkness inside the shop. When they finally did, I saw that the man behind the counter was watching me curiously.

The shop was filled with what I would expect from a pawn shop. Electronics like TVs and computers, jewelry in a glass case, musical instruments, and a huge collection of DVDs. I even saw a line of lawnmowers in the back of the store.

I bypassed all of this and went straight to the man that was waiting. He was tall, with wavy silver hair, and when he grinned at me, I could see that he was missing a tooth.

"What can I do for ya?" he asked.

"I want to pawn this." I held out the jewelry box. The man, whose name tag identified him as Carl, took it from me. He pulled out a loupe magnifying glass and opened up the box to reveal my engagement ring and wedding ring.

They were a matching set that Jeff had designed for us, so they were one of a kind. The engagement ring had a large princess-cut diamond surrounded by twelve tiny round diamonds. The wedding ring matched, the gold band holding six more of the tiny round diamonds. It was gorgeous, but not really my style. It was too big, too flashy. I wasn't a fan of showing off like Jeff was. Of course, he insisted that I wear it constantly. I had only taken the set off when cooking or showering. If I forgot to put them back on immediately after those activities, I was accused of being a whore and trying to attract men by posing as if I'm single. It didn't matter that I hardly ever left the house alone, and he probably had people watching me.

Carl held each ring up, peering at them through the loupe for a long time. I watched silently, wishing that I was spending my lunch break eating something instead of dealing with this.

"I'll give you thirty-five hundred for them," he said. I scoffed, I couldn't help myself.

"I know for a fact that those rings are worth twenty thousand dollars," I argued. "Thirty-five hundred is insultingly low."

"It's the best I can do," he said, handing the box back over.

I took it and headed for the door. If I had to, I'd sell it online or something.

I was almost to the door when he called out, " Okay, okay. I can go a little higher."

I turned back around. "Eight thousand."

Carl laughed, "No way. I'll do four."

"Six."

"Five, and that's it."

It wasn't nearly as much as I hoped to get, but it would cover the fake IDs. That was what really mattered.

"Deal."

I completed the paperwork and walked out with the money ten minutes later. I would go by the bar to drop off the payment tonight.

THE NEXT DAY was my first Mommy and Me class. Dominic had been reluctant to agree to it, uncharacteristically whining and stomping his feet, but I talked him into participating.

"You all set for this?" Swole asked, coming to the yoga room where I was getting ready while Dominic did somersaults on his yoga mat to pass the time.

"I think so," I said. "It might be a little chaotic at first, depending on whether or not the kids cooperate, but I'm hoping that'll be part of the fun."

"Fingers crossed," Swole agreed. "By the way, the meth lab has been cleared out. I had a come-to-Jesus talk with your neighbor, strongly *suggesting* that she kick her man to the damn curb and making it clear that we'd be keeping an eye on her."

"So, you think it's safe to go back?"

"I think that I scared the hell out of her and Rage, that's the piece of shit that was cooking in the house where his girl and kid lived, doesn't want the kind of trouble that he'll have if he pulls this shit again in the same place."

I wasn't completely convinced, but I trusted Swole and was sure that if she tried to intimidate Talia, she succeeded. The woman could probably scare a demon.

"Thanks. I guess we'll go back tonight."

Or maybe tomorrow. We had been staying with Trainer for the last couple of days, and I was enjoying myself. It was nice to fall asleep in his arms every night and wake up to a freshly brewed pot of coffee every morning. He was thoughtful in a way that I'd never experienced before.

"Okay, I'll bring the dog by and drop him off then," Swole said before leaving.

The class started, and as I predicted, it wasn't quite the calm experience of my other lessons. But the kids seemed to have fun, and their moms got to practice poses the same as always. If we kept doing this weekly over time, it should become more routine and run more smoothly. But I still counted our first attempt as a success.

For the first time, I had a student in class that I knew. Elaine and her son Glenn attended. I hadn't seen her since the day that our sons had met at the library, but Dominic had a great time at her house. He talked about his new friend for days.

"This was a great idea," Elaine said at the end of the class. We had rolled up our yoga mats, and the rest of the class was leaving the room in good spirits. "I'm always looking for ways that Glenn can be more active. And yoga is so good for stress levels too."

"I'm glad to see you guys here," I said as we watched our boys chatting animatedly.

"You know, Glenn would love to have a sleepover. He's been talking about it since we had Dominic over for the day. Is it too last minute to maybe have one tonight?"

I looked at Dominic, the easy smile on his face and how relaxed he was. It was like he was with his best friend.

"You know what? That'd be great."

Elaine gave me her address so that I could drop

Dominic off after packing a bag. As she and Glenn left, I squatted next to Dominic.

"Hey, buddy. Do you *want* to stay the night with Glenn? I know it can be a lot of pressure when your friend's standing right there, but you've never spent a whole night away from me. Do you think you'll be okay?"

"Yeah, mom. I think it'll be fun. Did you know that Glenn has *hundreds* of Spider-man comics? It's so cool."

"That *sounds* cool," I smiled. "But if you get scared in the night at any time, even if it's three in the morning, have Elaine call me, and I'll come right over to get you, okay?"

"Okay," he agreed.

We left the fitness studio, stopping at the duplex for the first time since Swole had delivered the news of a volatile chemical lab in the neighbor's basement. We packed up an overnight bag, and I took Dominic to the address that Elaine gave me. I was unexpectedly emotional as we said goodbye for the evening. It hit me how fast he was growing up, and I wasn't sure that I liked it. It was one of those things that I couldn't do anything about, but it still bummed me out.

I had a plan for the evening. To thank Trainer for being so great and letting us stay with him, I was going to make him dinner at his place. An electric ball of anticipation gathered in my stomach. This would be the first time we were alone together since our stolen time in my car behind the fitness center. I wanted to take things further tonight.

I knew that Trainer had a meeting with the Outlaw Souls tonight, so I sent him a text message, telling him to meet me at my place afterward.

I stopped at the grocery store and bought a couple of steaks. I wasn't sure what Trainer's favorite food was, but I figured I couldn't go wrong with Ribeyes.

It felt weird to be back at my house, even though I was

only gone a couple of days. Without Dominic and Trainer, it felt too empty. It was lonely, even with Gizmo there. I needed some noise. So I turned on some music on my phone while I cooked. My dad had always been into older rock bands - Styx, Genesis, Rush - and growing up listening to that stuff had made me a fan too. So, I was dancing around my kitchen barefoot with a pair of tongs in my hand while the steaks sizzled in the pan and singing *I Can't Dance* when the music suddenly cut out, and the phone rang.

I answered it without even thinking to look at the caller ID. So few people had my number that it didn't seem necessary.

"Hello?"

"Hello, Eve."

Time seemed to freeze as cold fear took a hold of me. My blood pounded in my ears, and I couldn't breathe.

"Nothing to say to your husband?" Jeff's voice was too soft. It reminded me of the calm before the storm. Bad things were coming. "I'm disappointed."

He was always disappointed. I couldn't do anything right in his eyes.

"H-how did you get this number?" I asked, my voice strangled. I hated that the fear was so clear in my voice. I wanted to be stronger.

"You didn't make it easy. I'll say that much. But giving your new phone number to Olivia was a stupid mistake."

"Is she okay? What did you do to her?"

Olivia was Dominic's personal tutor. Jeff wouldn't let him go to a public school where he could actually make friends. Instead, he'd hired a private tutor to come to the house and teach Dominic there. She was the only friend I had, but I was so stuck under Jeff's thumb that we weren't free to be as close as I would have liked. The day that I left,

I bought my burner phone and gave her the number so that we could keep in touch. Jeff was right, it was a stupid mistake, but I had been feeling sad about completely abandoning my life as if Eve Donovan never even existed. So, I'd left one connection that I didn't imagine in a million years Jeff would be able to find.

"Oh, she's fine. Very concerned about you and Dominic, though. After all, you're so unstable and have all that history of mental health problems."

"What?" I had no idea what he was talking about. I didn't have a history like that.

"That's what I told her, you dumb cow." There was the familiar anger.

Damn it. I should have told Olivia everything so she wouldn't fall for that. All I had told her was that things weren't working out between us and that I was scared of him. Jeff could be so damn charming I should have known he'd convince her of something like this.

"What do you want, Jeff?" I asked, lowering myself in a dining room chair because my legs were trembling.

"What do I want?" he repeated, his voice coated with rage. "I want my goddamn wife to know her place. I want you to get back here where you belong and beg me to forgive you. I want my son back-"

"No," I interrupted. It must have shocked him because he fell silent. "You'll never get Dominic back, do you hear me? He deserves so much better, and he's going to get it."

"You think he deserves to be stuck with *you*? You're worthless. I swear, you can't do a thing right, but you think you're fit to raise him on your own? You don't even have any skills. How will you get a job and support the two of you? *I* have the money to take care of the boy."

"Raising a child is about a hell of a lot more than money. He needs love, something that you're incapable of."

"He is mine," Jeff snapped. "You both are. You belong to me. Do you understand that? I OWN you!"

By the end, he was yelling and had to pull the phone away from my ear. "Leave us alone," I shouted too, my emotions overpowering my ability to even attempt a real conversation.

"Never. I'll never leave you alone because your mine, Eve. I'll find you and drag you back here where you belong."

I couldn't stand to listen to another word, so I chucked my phone across the room as hard as I could. It bounced off the wall and hit the floor in two pieces.

My head was spinning, and the longer I sat there, the closer I got to panic. I had an idea that he would still be looking for me, but it was different to hear it in his voice. He sounded so sure of himself.

I had to get the hell out of here. Pain ripped through my heart at the thought of leaving, but I had to. What if I'd messed up in some other way, and he could find me? The feeling of safety I'd been clinging to since I'd arrived felt like an illusion now. I was in danger. Dominic was in danger.

That got me moving. Standing from the table, I rushed upstairs and started packing. We needed to leave tonight.

NINETEEN
TRAINER

When Swole told me earlier in the day that Erica could move back into her apartment, I was less than pleased. I liked having her and Dominic around. My apartment was way too small for it, but I knew I was going to miss sleeping with Erica in my arms.

So, when she texted me asking that I come to her place for dinner, I had been happy. When she mentioned that Dominic would be staying at a friend's house all night, I couldn't fucking wait. It was well past time for us to take things to the next level physically.

That was my mindset when I arrived at Erica's house. The sun had just gone down, and it was a humid evening. The wind helped to keep me cool when the bike was in motion, but as soon as I parked, the sticky heat clung to my skin. I whipped my helmet off and walked up the porch steps. I hesitated at the door, not sure if I should knock, but in the end, I decided against it. She was expecting me, after all.

As soon as I walked in, the smell of burning meat

greeted me. I frowned. Walking toward the kitchen, I saw a haze in the air just before the smoke detector in the kitchen started going off.

"Shit," I mumbled. Hurrying to the stove, I used the oven mitt to grab a pan with a couple of charred steaks and move it off the heat. I turned up the fan on the hood and took the battery out of the annoying smoke detector.

Where the hell was Erica?

"Erica?" I yelled out.

Something was seriously wrong here. I became even more certain of that fact when I walked out into the dining room and saw her phone on the floor in pieces. Tendrils of panic started to take hold of me.

"Erica!" I shouted louder as I started to climb the stairs.

"Trainer?" I felt a small relief at the sound of her voice, but it wasn't enough to erase my concerns. She also sounded off somehow.

At the top of the stairs, I turned left, straight into her room. What I saw there stopped me dead in my tracks.

She was fucking *packing*. There were two suitcases open on the bed, and she was throwing things into them in a frenzy. I could see that her hands were shaking, and when she looked at me, her eyes looked crazed. It reminded me of a cornered animal.

"What the hell is going on?"

"I have to go," she said, her voice just as shaky as her hands. "I'm sorry, really. I wanted to stay to make this work, but I don't have that luxury. I married the wrong man, and now I'll pay for it forever."

"What happened?"

"I have to go," she repeated. I wasn't even sure that she was hearing me. She was so freaked out.

I stepped into the room, my strides long and steady as I drew closer to her. I rounded the bed until I was standing in front of her. I put my hands on her shoulders, stopping her from moving back and forth to and from the closet.

"What happened today? Why are you so freaked out?"

Erica looked up at me, taking a deep, shuddering breath. "He called me."

"Jeff?"

She gulped and nodded.

"What did he say?"

"He's coming to get me."

"He knows where you are?"

"I don't think so, not yet. If he did, he wouldn't have bothered to call."

"I don't understand. If he doesn't know where you are, why are you so freaked out? It sounds like an empty threat to me."

Erica shook her head and stepped backward, out of my reach. I could have followed, but I wasn't going to force the issue, not when she was feeling attacked already.

"You don't get it. You don't know him."

"No, I don't. But I do know that you're not going to have much of a life if you keep running like this. And neither will Dominic."

"I have to keep him safe," she said the words like a mantra. Then, she returned to stripping her closet of its contents.

"You can do that here. Come on, Erica, you're overreacting."

Her back was to me when she froze in place, dropping the clothing she had been holding to the floor at her feet. With her back ramrod straight and her face painted in lines of fury, she turned and looked at me.

"Overreacting? OVERREACTING? Who do you think you are? Mister Big, Tough, Biker Dude thinks he's seen it all and knows everything. Well, tell me, did you know that I've had broken ribs six times? Or that when we first met, there were black and blue bruises up and down my back? Or that Dominic used to have nightmares every night that I died?"

Every word she spoke was fuel for the fire within me. Jeff had better hope that I never met him in person. The most powerful protective instinct I'd ever experienced made me want to wrap her in my arms and never let go. I couldn't let anything like that happen to her or Dominic ever again.

"So, think twice next time you try to tell me how to feel about my husband." God, I hated that they were still married. "If I don't leave tonight, I'm basically taking a stand here. I'm choosing to stop running, and I don't think I can do that. I don't think I'm strong enough, damn it."

With every word she spoke, the anger seeped out of her, leaving a deep-rooted fear behind.

"I believe in you," I said, brushing a strand of hair off of her forehead. "And I'm here for you."

Erica shook her head. "I can't ask you to do that. This is my fight."

"And you're my girl," I argued. "Aren't you?"

Erica looked up into my eyes, and the atmosphere in the room shifted to something else. Electricity crackled between us, invisible but effective. Without overthinking it, I pulled her body into mine, taking her lips in a bruising kiss. I poured everything I was feeling for her into it, trying to tell without words how much her packing up to leave scared me and how much I cared about her.

Erica's hands explored my body freely, traveling under my shirt, where she traced my abs with her fingers before running her flat palms over my pecs. Then, she just pulled the shirt right off, getting it out of the way. It was hot as hell that she was taking the lead, doing what she wanted, and letting me know that she liked my body with the way that she couldn't stop touching it.

Breaking our kiss briefly, I knocked the half-full suitcases onto the floor before guiding her backward until she was sitting on the edge of the bed. She reached out and grabbed my belt buckle, pulling me forward until my hard erection was only inches from her face where it hid behind my zipper.

"I told you that it would be your turn this time," she said, licking her lips slowly.

I was so hard for her that it was almost painful. I watched as she used her nimble fingers to unbuckle my pants and open them. When she shoved them down, the only thing keeping my cock contained was the thin fabric of my boxers.

Erica brought both hands up on either side of my hips and gripped the waistband. Keeping her eyes on the prize, she pulled down my boxers, and my aching erection jutted out toward her face. She gasped, and I felt the intake of air on the tip because she was so close. It was a sweet torture.

The next thing I knew, she had wrapped her hand firmly around it and started stroking me slow and steady. Just when I got used to that, she leaned in and placed a kiss on the tip. I felt a quick zap of pleasure, but I needed so much more.

"Erica, fuck. Please, baby. Don't torture me."

She must have been waiting for me to ask because as soon as the words were out of my mouth, she took me into her mouth. Erica went as deep as she could right off the bat, and my breath left my lungs in a burst of pleasure. She kept her hand at the base and moved it up and down with her mouth. It wasn't long before waves of pleasure radiated from her efforts, and I felt myself building up to a climax.

"Stop," I said breathlessly. She did, looking up at me with confusion. "I've got to come inside you, baby. And I don't mean in that pretty little mouth of yours. Not this time."

I kicked off my jeans and boxers, but stopped long enough to grab my wallet and the condom that I always kept in there. Pressing another kiss to Erica's lips, I moved forward onto the bed. I made quick work of removing the dress she was wearing, only to stop and stare at the lingerie underneath. Black lace covered her most private areas, but not well enough to truly hide them. I could still see bare flesh peeking out and the outline of two very erect nipples.

I wanted to take my time to explore every inch of her with my tongue, but I didn't think I could wait another second to be inside of her. Besides, we'd have time for slow exploration later. We had all night, after all.

I pulled her panties off and placed my hand at her entrance to find that she was wet and ready for me.

"Oh my, you want this, don't you?" I asked, dipping a finger inside and watching her squirm. "Have you been fantasizing about this like I have? Do you touch yourself when you think of me?"

Erica gasped and threw her head back as I pumped my finger in and out of her, but she didn't answer.

"I said, do you touch yourself when you think of me?" I repeated, dipping my head down to her chest, I lightly bit her nipple through her bra.

"Yes," she cried out.

I put my thumb on her clit and rubbed in time with my pumping finger. "Yes, what?"

"Yes, I touch myself while thinking about you," she admitted. There was a desperation in her voice, and I knew just what she was needy for.

I pulled my hand away, and she let out a soft cry of protest. I ripped open the condom and quickly rolled it on while she shed her bra. Lining myself up at her entrance, I kissed her, thrusting my tongue into her mouth at the same time that I drove my hips forward, burying myself inside her.

She gripped my shoulders so tightly that I thought her fingernails might cut me open, but I didn't mind. I like a sharp little bite of pain to go with my pleasure. It just made everything feel even better.

I started to move in and out, slowly at first, but then building momentum until I was pounding her into the mattress. She met me at every thrust, taking everything I had to give and crying out for more. Every gasp and moan was music to my ears, and I couldn't get enough of the way she shuddered with pleasure. She was so damn hot when she did that, and I wasn't sure how long I could stand it without coming.

But I was a big believer in ladies first. So, I gritted my teeth and kept going until a fine sheen of sweat coated both of our bodies.

"Oh my god, Trainer. I'm... I'm... Fuck, I'm coming. Trainer!"

Erica's orgasm hit, and she screamed my name. It was fucking incredible to know that I had given her so much pleasure. Then, her tight, wet heat started to convulse around my cock, as if trying to milk it. That was it, no more holding back as I exploded. A primal, guttural sound escaped me as I let loose.

I collapsed onto the bed beside Erica afterward. All my strength left my body, sapped by the powerful climax I'd just experienced.

I gathered Erica into my arms and kissed her forehead. We laid there quietly for several minutes, basking in the afterglow of our union. I was just thinking that I needed to go into the bathroom and deal with the condom when Erica sat up in bed with a gasp.

"Oh, shit. The steaks!"

She started to scramble out of bed, but I reached out and stopped her. "Don't worry, I took care of that when I came in. I moved them off the heat, or what was left of them, anyway, and I turned the oven off.

"Oh my god, I can't believe I did that." She lowered her head and rubbed her temples.

"Well, you were pretty shaken up," I reasoned.

"Yeah," she agreed, "There's still a part of me that thinks I should get out of here, run somewhere new, and hope he doesn't find me, but I can't be happy that way. I think that's why I fell to pieces when he called. I had let my guard down here and allowed myself happiness. I've been thinking about a future," she reached over and took my hand, intertwining our fingers. "Then, my ugly past came back up and reminded me that I can't move on until that's dealt with."

"So, what do you want to do?"

"I'll stay," she said, not sounding completely sure. "But I'm not sure what to do about Jeff, yet."

"You'll figure it out. And I'll be here to support you." It was on the tip of my tongue to say three little words that were way too early. I surprised even myself with that one, but it felt right somehow.

Erica and I salvaged what we could of dinner, eating in bed, and talking about anything that wasn't Jeff. Erica wanted an escape, and I gave it to her. Then later, I gave myself a treat by taking my time with her and exploring her whole body with my mouth and hands. She was amazing.

TWENTY

ERICA

I was starting to think that I might love Trainer. I told myself that I was crazy, that it was too soon, but that didn't change the way that my heart stuttered just from being near him. There was no stopping these feelings. I was crazy about him. The evidence was in what happened last night. I didn't think anyone else in the world could have cut through my panic the way he did.

I woke up first this morning, which had never happened before. In the days that I had been staying at Trainer's apartment, he woke up before me every day. I assumed he was one of those morning people that I would never understand.

When I turned over in bed and saw that he was still out like a light, I took a few minutes to study his face. His naturally tanned skin was smooth, and his lips plump. His beard was full, but he kept it clean and trimmed. I never would have thought that I would be attracted to a bearded man, as it had never been my type before, but it worked for him, adding to the sexy biker vibe that he had going on. I smiled as I watched him. He looked so peaceful in his sleep. It almost made him look younger even.

He was still naked from our activities the night before, and I let my eyes wander down his chest, noting a long, thin scar on his right pectoral. I wondered what it was. A knife wound, maybe? His full sleeve tattoo actually started on his chest as a series of swirls and curves that became tighter and interlocked together along his shoulder. Then shapes started to form along his bicep. I saw motorcycles, skulls, the Outlaw Souls logo, and what looked like tools, maybe. The images were all in black and grey, and they ended at his wrist. The more I looked at it, the more I saw.

"What are you staring at so intently?" Trainer asked, startling me. He had woken up at some point.

I smiled. "Just trying to get a good look in the light of day," I said, tracing the edge of a skull on his forearm with the tip of my finger. "What would you think if I got a tattoo?"

"That'd be fucking hot."

"Does it hurt really bad?"

"Depends on where you get it," he said, talking through a yawn. "I'm not going to lie, around the elbow hurt like a bitch."

He held up his arm, showing me a starburst pattern at his elbow.

"I was thinking that I should get something significant to me. Like the word perseverance along my wrist maybe. Some kind of reminder of what I've been through and that I'm stronger for it."

I did feel that way, even though I'd had a moment of weakness last night. The fact was that I wasn't the same woman that stuck around for years in that shitty situation.

"You just have to make sure you'll be happy with it. They're forever, ya know."

We got out of bed. I was supposed to pick Dominic up at Elaine's house at ten, so I had an hour until I had to leave. Trainer and I both needed a shower, so we got in together, but it was a while before any proper cleaning was done. I couldn't believe how much I wanted this man after we'd had sex twice last night. I'd never experienced that before. My only other sexual partner had been Jeff, but even before I realized what a scumbag he was, I didn't want him like this. And the sex was incomparable. Jeff was selfish, and Trainer was... *earth-shattering.*

The word love crossed my mind again, and I tried to ignore it. I had to find a way to get Jeff to leave me alone before I could allow myself to go there.

When we went downstairs, I picked up the broken pieces of my phone. I hoped with all my heart that Dominic didn't try to call me to pick him up last night. I hadn't been thinking about that when I broke the damn thing. In fact, I hadn't had a rational thought at all until Trainer showed up. It was amazing what effect fear could have on the mind.

I threw the cell phone away and took Gizmo outside to use the bathroom. While Trainer got the coffee pot going. The back porch was much like the front in that it was one big porch divided in half. I was standing on my half when Talia came outside, choosing to grab a cigarette on the back porch this time.

"You got a dog, huh?" she asked. She looked like hell, with dark circles under her eyes, and her clothes looked dirty.

"Yeah, for my son."

"Ugly little thing." She was eyeing his scars with distaste.

I frowned, but I didn't want to get pulled into an argument with her, so I didn't respond. I just wanted Gizmo to hurry up and pick a spot to poop so I could go inside and grab a cup of coffee before leaving to pick up Dominic.

"I saw that bike out front. So, your fucking one of those Outlaw Souls, huh?"

"I'm dating one of them, yes."

"They think they're so great, busting up in my house like they have a right to be here. They don't. They think they can act like the damn police in La Playa."

I had no idea what she was talking about. Swole had told me about the meth lab and that their rivals were responsible, but that was it.

"I'm just saying," she went on, "I didn't have problems like this before you moved in."

"I didn't rat you out, if that's what you're thinking," I said tiredly. I had bigger things to worry about right now. "I didn't even know you were doing that stuff over there."

"*I* wasn't doing anything. It was Rage. The basement was his man cave."

"Rage? Is that your boyfriend's nickname or something?"

"He's not my boyfriend anymore," she spat bitterly. "He was pissed when I told him that his stash was gone."

"So, you're not mad that he did this?" I asked incredulously. I was furious that my child was put in danger, and I didn't even have a personal relationship with the man. She should be pissed and feel betrayed.

"You know what? I think you're a nosy bitch. Tell your damn friends to leave me alone."

Talia took a last drag off her cigarette before flicking it into the grass. *Lovely.*

I watched as she turned her back on me and strutted

into her half of the house. A nudge against my calf brought my attention to Gizmo, who was sitting on the porch beside me, wagging his tail.

"That was weird. Huh, boy?" I bent down and patted his head. "I guess some people just need someone to blame when their life implodes."

"Talking to yourself?" Trainer asked from the doorway of the backdoor. He was shirtless and looking at me with a little half-smile.

"Talking to my good friend, Gizmo," I replied. "Now, I need to go get Dominic."

"And I need to meet a buyer for the Triumph Bonneville I just finished restoring."

I came back into the house with Gizmo trailing behind. "Then, we'll meet here for dinner tonight?"

It wasn't really a question. Things had changed in our relationship last night. I wasn't sure if it was because we'd finally moved forward physically or because I had accepted that I was going to stay in La Playa no matter what. Either way, we weren't dating casually anymore.

"I can grab a pizza or something," he suggested.

"Mama Tammy was right, you don't cook anything, do you?"

"Nope."

I smiled and shook my head. "Let's go to Tiny's then. Dominic and I can meet you at six-thirty."

"It's a date," he said, kissing my lips before heading upstairs to finish getting dressed.

I pushed all thoughts of Talia out of my mind as I poured a cup of coffee into my travel mug. Instead, I thought about Jeff. Hearing from him last night was a shock, and his threats were causing lingering anxiety, but I couldn't live in fear any longer. He might have money and resources, but he was only human.

I had to abandon thoughts of him as some kind of boogie monster. That was giving him too much credit.

TWENTY-ONE

TRAINER

"Are you whistling?" Swole asked as she came into the garage where I was working on my bike. It was almost due for a tune-up, and I liked to stay on top of that. It was basic motorcycle maintenance.

"Don't know what you're talking about," I said without looking up at her. I just hoped that she didn't recognize what I had been whistling.

"Wasn't that something from a video game? Mario, maybe?"

Yes, it was. The Bowser's castle music was stuck in my head all morning.

"It's Dominic's favorite video game," I said. "And he's really good at it."

"Typical seven-year-old."

"He's almost eight, actually," I told her. "Next month. Erica wants to have a party."

Swole stopped on the other side of my bike and looked down at me with a bemused expression.

"What?" I asked snippily.

"You, that's what. You're crazy about those two."

Yeah, I was. But it didn't exactly feel manly to admit it. I'd catch shit from the single guys in the club if they caught me swooning like this.

"Why are you here?" I asked, not even trying to pretend I wasn't changing the subject.

"I brought my bike. I'm noticing a squeak in the front brake. It seems to be working fine, but the sound can't be a good thing."

"No, probably not."

Swole was one of the few members that didn't work on her bike. She'd change the oil, or something else that was basic, but anything else was handled by me or Ryder. Standing from my crouched position beside the bike, I walked over and grabbed a couple of beers from the mini-fridge. Popping the tops off, I handed one to Swole.

"I'll take a look. Might not get to it, until tomorrow though. I've got plans this evening."

"Hot date?" Swole smirked.

"Why are you giving me a hard time?" I asked, exasperated.

"I'm not, asshole." Swole rolled her eyes at me. "I like Erica. You're a good match."

"Oh."

"Yeah. Don't be so damn defensive. There's nothing to be embarrassed about."

"I'm not embarrassed," I said. It was true. I just spent a lot of time with lifelong bachelors that disparaged anyone that settled down. Moves was a prime example. He'd often given Ryder shit about settling for one woman when there were so many to pick from in La Playa.

As usual, Swole seemed to understand where my mind was at without me having to say a word. "Fuck anyone that gives you a hard time. You find your happiness and take it. You'll be a better man for it."

"You think so?" I asked, taking a big swig of my beer.

"Hell, yeah. You think I'm a bitch now? You shoulda seen me before Tammy made an honest woman outta me."

I laughed. "Thank God for good women."

"Amen to that," she said, and we drank together.

I WALKED into Tiny's and spotted Hawk at a table by the door. He was working his way through a mountain of food, which was so typical of him. He was a workaholic, the type to get hyper-focused on whatever he was doing and forget to eat until he was starving. I'd told him a million times that it was unhealthy as hell, but he was a stubborn ox and would continue to do whatever he pleased.

I walked up to the counter and ordered a couple of meals to-go. I was supposed to meet Erica and Dominic at the park soon, and it seemed like a good idea to bring dinner. After being told the food would take fifteen minutes, I doubled back and took a seat at Hawk's table.

"What are you up to?" he asked after swallowing a mouthful of food.

"Picking up dinner."

"Why not just eat here?" he gestured to the diner around us. "The décor not to your liking?"

"I'm meeting someone. A woman."

"Anyone, I know?"

"Erica Mills. Have you met her yet? She teaches yoga at the fitness center."

I saw something like surprise flash through Hawk's eyes. He definitely knew who I was talking about.

"Erica... Erica..." he looked thoughtful. I couldn't shake the feeling that was an act, but I let him play it that way, for now. "Brown hair? Kid? Rockin' body?"

"Yes, to all three."

Hawk let out a low whistle. "Damn, you're hittin' that? You're a lucky son of a bitch."

"Yeah, I am." I couldn't help smiling.

"Is it serious?" he asked, a little too casually.

"Yes." The cagey feeling I'd had when talking to Swole disappeared now as I realized that Hawk might be interested in Erica too. I needed to stake a claim now. "She's mine."

"Interesting." Hawk didn't seem bothered by my words. He just pierced me with a speculative look.

The waitress brought my order to the table in a couple of white plastic bags. I stood. "Catch you at The Blue Dog for the fight tomorrow night?" I asked.

"I'll be there."

The park Erica wanted to meet at was less than a mile from her house. When I asked her why she wanted to go there, she told me that it was a nice day and Dominic could use the exercise. Before I met her, I wouldn't have thought that I would find responsible parenting to be an attractive feature, but I liked how dedicated she was to her son. It showed what a good woman she was.

I hadn't been to this park before, it wasn't exactly my normal hangout, but I lucked out when I saw that there was a shelter space with wooden picnic benches. Grabbing the food out of the passenger seat of my truck, I shrugged out of my jacket. The leather was great to protect from potential road rash, but on a sunny day like this, it was too hot for hanging around outside.

Erica was already sitting at a picnic table with a can of

soda in her hand. There was a happy smile on her face as she watched Dominic running around, climbing like a monkey on the playground equipment. She was so damn beautiful. Even in the shade, she seemed to shine somehow, as if her inner beauty was showing through.

When she spotted me walking her way, she waved me over, ignoring the two other mothers sitting nearby that shot me pensive looks. I was used to it. People thought I was scary. It was nothing but a superficial assessment. I tried not to take it personally. I was just glad that Erica either didn't notice or didn't care.

"You brought food?" she asked as I sat both bags down on the table.

"Dinner," I said, first straddling the bench seat across from her, then swinging my leg over and sitting properly. "From Tiny's."

"You're the best."

"How was your day?" I asked.

She chatted about her day while I set up the food, telling me about her yoga classes and the reading she'd done on meditation going hand-in-hand with her work. It was nothing especially significant, but I liked listening to her. It was nice to have someone to talk to about nothing over dinner. I wasn't sure how I'd lasted so many years eating my meals alone and silent.

Dominic joined us as soon as he saw the food laid out on the table. "Are the chicken tenders for me?" he asked excitedly.

"Yep. Unless you want my catfish?" I asked jokingly. I'd gotten to know him well enough to know that the only fish he would eat was tuna casserole. He was a typical picky kid, but I figured I'd be safe going with chicken tenders and fries. What kid didn't like that?

"Ew," he grimaced and stuck out his tongue.

"Chicken, it is." I placed the food in front of him, then gave Erica hers. "And for the lady."

"Grilled chicken breast. How do you remember these things?"

I shrugged. "It sounds like a lame dating profile characteristic, but I really am a good listener."

"Do you enjoy walks on the beach, too?" she teased.

"Very funny. As a matter of fact, I do *not*."

"What?" Dominic asked around a mouthful of food. "Who doesn't like the beach?"

"A man with a big old beard that had a tendency to trap sand."

"No beach, huh?" Erica asked, shaking her head. "And here I thought you might just be perfect."

"Afraid not," I said, but the sentiment made something warm fill my chest.

Dominic spent the entire time we were eating talking about his day, telling me stories about children at his daycare and TV shows he liked watching. I found that he was usually rather repetitive, but I didn't mind. Erica was a real champion, though. She listened to every word that he said, asking follow-up questions and making him seem like the most interesting person on earth. The woman had kid-listening skills.

"Hey, Trainer? Do you want to play catch with me? I brought my baseball and an extra glove."

We had just finished eating, and I would have preferred to digest for a bit while sitting with Erica, but I couldn't say no to an offer like that.

"Sure thing." I took the spare glove from him. It was an adult-sized glove, but still a little small for me. I shoved my hand into it as best as I could and followed him to a patch of grass beside the playground. We were in the shade of a large tree, and I had a surreal moment as I looked around at the happy children and the idyllic surroundings. This wasn't my kind of thing normally, but maybe it could be.

Dominic and I stood about twenty feet apart, and I held up my glove.

"Okay, throw it right to me."

Dominic's first throw went wide, and I had to chase it down. When I returned to my spot, he was staring at the ground, looking like he was close to tears.

What the fuck?

I jogged over to him and knelt at eye level. "What's wrong?"

"I didn't mean to do that," he said miserably.

I was confused. Why was he so upset? One wide throw wasn't a reason to go to pieces.

Then, I looked up and met Erica's concerned gaze. Suddenly, I felt like an idiot. It was his dad, that was the reason he was so upset. An ugly hatred for a man I didn't even know churned in my belly.

"Hey, listen to me. I don't mind. You can throw them all like that, and I'll just chase 'em down. I could probably use the exercise." Dominic laughed. It wasn't a completely joyful sound, but it was better than the misery he was showing before. I handed him the ball. "Here. Try again."

I went back to my position, and Dominic threw again. This time it came right to me.

"Good job."

Dominic smiled. We threw the ball back and forth a few more times, getting into a rhythm.

"You know, I've never done this before," I told him.

"Never?" he asked, amazed.

"Nope."

"My dad made me do it," he said, frowning. "He always wanted me to be an athlete."

I thought about his words for a moment. The next time he threw the ball, I caught and held it.

"So, do you not enjoy this?"

"I'm having fun with you," he said quickly.

"I'm having fun with you, too." I walked closer to him, until only a few feet separated us. "But we can have fun doing something else."

"Dad always said that when I went to the park, I had to practice playing ball. That's why I brought these," he gestured to the gloves.

"Well, we've practiced. What else would you like to do?"

"I like to look for bugs."

He looked thoroughly embarrassed as he admitted it to me, which made me believe that his father probably ridiculed that interest.

"Bugs, huh? You like to study them and all that?"

"Yeah," he agreed. "I checked out a book from the library once all about them. My mom helped me make paper butterflies and moths to hang in my room based on the pictures in the book, but dad didn't like them."

I wanted to change the subject from his dad, despite the anger I felt every time Dominic mentioned the man.

"Well, bug hunting sounds like fun to me. Want to get your mom in on it?"

"Yeah!"

Dominic ran off to Erica as fast as his little legs would carry him. His excitement was obvious, and I didn't understand how his dad could have stifled such a thing.

There were trees surrounding the outskirts of the park, and the three of us headed that way. We spent the next hour hunting for bugs to observe, finding ladybugs, a praying mantis, and two butterflies. Dominic loved it. I couldn't help thinking that we were like a family, and it felt good.

It reminded me of the days that they'd stayed at my apartment. It was great, and I missed it. By the time we left the park at dusk, I was thinking it might be a good idea to ask Erica to move in with me when the time was right.

Dominic was exhausted by the time we returned to the duplex. Erica said it was a little early for his bedtime, but he seemed happy to go to bed. Erica was only in his room for ten minutes, and by the time she came out, he was already asleep.

"Thanks for that today," she said, taking a seat beside me on her couch. "The whole insect thing used to be a big interest of his, but he hasn't talked about it in a while. I thought he had just moved on to something else, the way kids do, but I guess it was Jeff's influence. I should have known."

"I'm glad that he had a good time. But I'm not going to lie. I'm even happier that I get you to myself for a bit."

I trailed my fingers along her bare arm, smirking as I watched her shiver. Her eyes met mine, and her green orbs were liquid pools of desire. I let my lust take over, propelling me forward to take her mouth in a hard kiss. The couch creaked under my weight as I shifted my position, pulling my shirt over my head. Erica's small hands ran over my bare skin, tracing my muscles, going lower and lower until she dipped her fingers into the waistband of my jeans.

I broke our kiss to trail my lips along her jawline and down her neck. She tasted so sweet, and I needed more.

Our limbs became a flurry of movement as we stripped each other, pulling and touching until we were both naked.

The only light in the room came from a lamp, and her pale skin was beautifully illuminated in the faint glow. I was sitting on the edge of the couch while she stood before me. My mouth went to her chest, desperate to lick and suck. Erica threw her head back, gasping, but keeping quiet. We were both aware that there was a child sleeping upstairs, and this would have to be a silent fuck. For me, that knowledge made it hotter, knowing that she was going to have to suppress moans of deep pleasure caused my cock to throb.

God, I was like a horny adolescent again, a slave to the needs of my body. She brought that out of me, a need that I hadn't felt in so long. Like I might die if I didn't take her.

I grabbed her ass as I switched my mouth to her other nipple, teasing it with my tongue until it was hard, then biting it very lightly. Erica's hands had tightened on my shoulders as she rotated her hips, as if searching for something to relieve the ache between her legs.

I finally pulled away from her chest to tell her to get on her hands and knees, but she didn't give me a chance. With surprising strength, she used the palm of her hand to push against my chest until I was leaned against the back of the couch. Then, she was straddling me.

"I think I'll go for a wild ride tonight," she said, and I bucked my hips to show her just how wild it could get.

She kissed me, softer this time, but her tongue went right into my mouth, tasting me as it swirled around my own. While I was tongue-tied, she reached down between us and gripped my cock. Her touch was warm and soft, but it felt like I'd been zapped by electricity as tingling ran up my spine. A single drop of liquid appeared at the tip, and Erica gathered it up with her thumb before rubbing it around the head of my erection, making me slick and so ready for her. I silently thanked God that she started the birth control pill, so there didn't have to be anything separating us.

"Erica, I need you, baby. Right fucking now."

She didn't need to be told twice. Lifting her hips, she positioned herself over my quivering cock. I liked this take charge thing she had going on, so I grabbed ahold of the couch cushions on either side of me and held on, letting her do whatever she wanted to me. I wanted her to unleash her passion for me.

Holding herself steady by hanging onto the back of the couch, she lowered herself onto me slowly, stretching herself as she took my entire length in one go. I ground my teeth to keep from groaning loudly, my chest pumping up and down with my heavy breathing.

The feeling of her warm pussy was like coming home.

She didn't give me much time to brace myself before she started moving. It was a wild ride, indeed. Erica bounced herself up and down on top of me with such vigor that her breasts bounced in my face.

Fuck. How could one woman be this hot?

She didn't even have to try, the sexiness poured out of her. It was in the way she rocked her hips and bit her lip, the way her breathy moans were barely audible but still enough to heighten my pleasure even further. It was in the way her tight channel got wetter and wetter as she got closer and closer to her orgasm.

Then, she did the final thing that pushed me right over the edge and free falling into a pool of ecstasy.

Dirty. Talk.

"Do you feel that, baby? The way that you fill me up with every thick inch," she was whispering in my ear as our pelvises slapped together repeatedly. "You make me want to come all over your cock."

"Erica," her name spilled from my mouth on the hiss as I lost all control. My climax took me, and I lost all sense of time and place. All I knew was pleasure, and it intensified as Erica found her release. I felt her core convulsing around me, and I had to grab her hips, just to ground myself, otherwise I felt like I might float away.

It was several minutes before my climax fully passed. I finally relaxed as Erica collapsed on my chest, her body curling into me. We were still connected at the hips, but even more importantly, I could feel the strongest emotional connection of my entire life. I didn't give a shit if it made me a sap. As I put my arms around the woman that had just completely rocked my world, I was sure that I had found *the one*.

TWENTY-TWO
ERICA

My fake IDs were ready. I'd missed a call from Hawk during one of my advanced yoga classes, but his voicemail informed me that he would be at The Blue Dog in the evening. So, after my last class of the day, I cleaned up quickly before walking across the street.

The Blue Dog looked the same as always; bikers at the bar, civilians playing pool, a basketball game on TV. I was starting to get used to being here by now and found it almost comfortable.

Hawk was easy to spot, sitting in the same corner as the day I met him. This time he was alone, and there was a sealed brown envelope on the table next to his beer. I sat down at the table across from him, and he slid the envelope over.

"It's all there," he said, taking a swig of his beer. "Driver's licenses, passports, even social security cards."

I opened the envelope and pulled out the contents. He was right. It was all here, and it looked legit.

"This will hold up to scrutiny from cops? Employers?" I

asked, staring down at my smiling face on the driver's license.

"Yep. You're golden."

I smiled. This was exactly what I needed, and well worth the price. I could officially live as Erica Mills now. I could stay in La Playa.

"Thanks," I said, starting to stand.

"Just curious," Hawk said before I got the chance to walk away. "Does Trainer know about this?"

I was surprised by his question. He must have seen me around the Outlaw Souls apartment complex when we were staying with Trainer. Had he talked to his friend in the club about me? I felt almost giddy at the thought, like a lovesick teenager.

"About the fake IDs?" I asked.

"That Erica Mills isn't your real name. I don't need to know what you're running from, but he should."

"He does," I said. "He's the only one who knows, so-"

"Don't worry about me. I don't air other people's shit."

That was good to know.

"See you around," I said.

Walking out of The Blue Dog, I gripped the brown envelope tightly in my hand. This was my ticket to freedom. It should keep Jeff from finding us.

I PICKED Dominic up from the babysitter and listened to him tell me all about his day on the way home.

"Hey, Dominic," I waited until there was a lull in his dialogue to get his attention. "How would you like to go to public school this fall?"

"Really?" he asked brightly. "We're going to stay here?"

"I think so." I didn't want to make any promises.

"Can I get a Spider-man backpack?"

I chuckled. "Sure."

"Then, yeah. I wanna go."

"I'll look into getting you registered."

I pulled up in front of the duplex, letting Dominic go in ahead of me. I dropped my gym bag next to the door, resolving to go through it later and do a load of laundry.

"Can I have a snack?" Dominic asked, already heading toward the kitchen.

"Something small, like an apple. I don't want you filling up on junk and ruining your dinner."

I had stopped walking halfway through the living room. Something was off. I couldn't quite put my finger on what it was at first, but for some reason, there was trepidation in my steps, fueled by a powerful sense of unease.

Finally, I realized that the things in the living room, the knick-knacks and picture frames, had all been moved slightly. They were still technically in the same spot, like the photo of Dominic and I on the coffee table, but they were slightly altered. The picture was facing the wrong direction. Someone had been in my home and moved my things.

"Mom?"

Dominic's voice held undisguised panic. I snapped my head in his direction and saw that he was frozen in the kitchen doorway, his back to me as he stared into the room at something I couldn't see. I flat-out ran to him, alarm bells going off in my head.

I didn't stop until I was standing in front of him, blocking Dominic from the thing in the kitchen that had him so scared. It was the thing I feared most.

My heart seemed to stop completely as I stood there,

staring at Jeff. He looked cool as a cucumber, watching me with the eyes of a predator as he leaned against my kitchen sink with his arms folded across his chest.

I wanted to run. The need was so strong that my hands shook, and my knees felt weak. But I couldn't get away, not when he was already inside my home. I heard Gizmo enter the kitchen behind us.

Some guard dog.

"Dominic, I need you to take the dog outside and stay with him until I tell you to come in." My voice was higher-pitched than normal, containing the faint edge of hysteria.

"But mom-"

"Now," I interrupted. "Go."

He did as I said, walking through the kitchen to the back door. There was a moment, when he passed by Jeff, that a deep-rooted fear engulfed me. Nothing was more terrifying to me than the possibility that Jeff could hurt Dominic the way he hurt me.

But Jeff let him go, staying in his leaning position against the kitchen sink the whole time until both Dominic and Gizmo were out the door. There was a sliver of relief amid my overwhelming anxiety. This was going to get ugly, and Dominic didn't need to see that.

"H-how did you find me?" I couldn't resist asking. I'd tried so hard to keep him off my trail.

Jeff gave me a smile that was so cold that I had to force myself not to flinch at the sight of it. "Do you remember when we got engaged?"

He paused, apparently wanting an actual answer.

"Yes," I replied shortly.

"And I told you that I had your rings designed just for you. You remember that?"

"Yes." What was he getting at here? Sure, he spent a

fortune on those rings for me, but he should know by now that his money wasn't enough to make me stick around.

"That makes them easy to recognize and track," he said, as if he were explaining something obvious. "When you pawned the rings, my PI found out. Then, he found *you*."

I swallowed thickly. I'd screwed up.

"You know, I always knew that you weren't too bright," Jeff continued, standing straight and coming toward me at a leisurely pace, as if he had no concerns in the world. I could only hope that his arrogance meant that he'd take longer to get violent, and maybe Trainer would come by in time to stop him. "But this shit you pulled, running away from me, hiding like this, was a whole new level of stupid."

I started to back away, so each forward step he took was mirrored by a backward step from me. I was desperate not to see the space between us disappear. We ended up in the dining room as I backed right out through the kitchen doorway.

"I had to run," I said, feeling the need to defend myself despite the knowledge that he'd never listen to reason. "I told you it was over so many times, and you wouldn't listen."

"You don't get to decide when it's over," he roared. His unsettling calm gave way to a rage that was scary but familiar.

I planted my feet as my anger surged forth. I'd suppressed all my anger and hatred for this man for years, telling myself that it was better to take what he dished out because fighting back just made it worse. Now, I was a different person. I was a strong woman that left an abusive man and started to build a new life for herself. I'd even found love with someone else.

I couldn't cower away from Jeff anymore. I wouldn't.

Planting my feet, I lifted my chin and tried to speak

confidently, "I *do* get to decide what I want from my life, and this isn't it. *You're* not it."

"You bitch. I don't know who you think you are, but I'll remind you that you're *my* wife. You belong to me."

"Despite what you think being married means, I'm not an object. I don't belong to anyone."

"You sound like a whore."

"I'm calling the cops," I said, reaching into my jeans to pull out my phone. I couldn't believe that I didn't do this immediately. I just got so caught up in the shock of seeing Jeff that I didn't think.

Jeff was enraged. Charging forward, he ripped the phone out of my hand and slammed it onto the ground. His heel ground it into the hardwood floor, and I bit back my despair. Without a way to communicate with the outside world. I was completely at his mercy.

"That was a new phone," I told him angrily, despite the pending danger he represented. I did back up several paces to create more distance, but I realized too late that there was a wall behind me. There was nowhere else to go.

He chuckled humorlessly. "Who cares? When we're home, I could buy you a thousand phones if I wanted."

"No, Jeff. I'm not going anywhere with you."

This was my line in the sand, and I wasn't budging. There was no going back to the life we had before.

"You never learn a lesson, do you?"

He was faster than I remembered. One minute, Jeff was standing five feet away. Then I blinked, and he was in front of me. Grabbing my arms above the elbow in a bruising grip, he shoved me back into the wall, knocking the breath out of my lungs. Jeff pinned me in place with his hands flat on the wall at each side of me.

"You can't get away from me," he snarled, his handsome

features distorted into something hateful and ugly. "I'll always find you and bring you back. You agreed to be together for the rest of our lives, and you don't get to change your mind about that."

"Get away from me," I said firmly while reaching out and pushing against his chest with all my strength. He was much stronger than I was, but the move must have taken him by surprise, because he stumbled back just enough to allow me to slip away from the wall.

"Get out," I demanded. "This is *my* home, and I don't want you here."

"That's enough," he snapped. I could see that his temper was rising, but I couldn't back down. "I'm getting Dominic, and we're all leaving."

No way.

I blocked his way back to the kitchen, folding my arms across my chest. Jeff smacked me across the face in one fluid movement, apparently abandoning his unspoken rule about leaving no marks that could be seen. My cheek stung at the contact, and he put enough force into it to knock me off-balance. I gasped, and my hand flew to my cheek, gingerly touching the sensitive skin there.

"I told you, *you never learn.* But I'm going to teach you the hard way."

I tried to fight him off, in a way that I hadn't for years, but it was no good. I found myself shoved and slapped as he unleashed his anger. He wrapped one of his hands around my throat and squeezed, cutting off my air until my vision started to darken, and I thought I might pass out. Desperately, I reached up and dragged my fingernails across his face, drawing blood and a curse from his lips as he let go. I staggered away from him into the living room, but I hadn't gone more than a couple of steps when Jeff was on me again.

Eventually, I ended up on the floor at his feet, and a swift kick to my ribs caused a sickening crunch, and a horrid pain bloomed. He'd definitely broken a couple of ribs with that move. I'd never experienced more than one of them fractured at a time. The resulting pain made me want to scream if only I could draw enough air into my lungs.

"Mom?"

Like a nightmare, I lifted my head and saw Dominic standing in the doorway, watching us with wide eyes. *Shit.*

"Get your shit packed," Jeff said in a tone that suggested there was no room for argument. "We're going home."

Dominic's dismayed expression turned to pure panic at those words.

"No," I croaked out. "Dominic, get the hell out of here."

"Shut up," Jeff growled, but I ignored it. I needed Dominic to get the hell out of here.

"Run," I told him, maintaining eye contact. "Leave the house right now. Don't come back."

Dominic only hesitated for a second. Then, he pivoted on his heel and raced back through the kitchen. I heard the back door slam into the wall as he ripped it open.

He was gone.

Thank God. I could endure whatever Jeff threw at me, but I didn't want him setting his sights on my son. As I watched, he gritted his teeth and started to follow Dominic. I tried to get up and follow, but the screaming pain in my side made it impossible to move fast enough. I looked around wildly before spotting the baseball glove that Dominic had discarded on the floor after playing catch with Trainer yesterday. Grabbing it, I found the baseball inside.

Generally, luck didn't appear to be on my side today,

but when I lobbed the baseball in Jeff's direction, it sailed through the air and hit Jeff right on the back of the head.

"Son of a bitch!" he yelled, his hand going to the back of his head. I could see that it hadn't even drawn blood, and was slightly disappointed, but at least I'd gotten his attention.

"You must truly be crazy," he said darkly as he advanced on me. I kicked out at him, to keep him away, the movement causing more pain in my ribs. He caught my foot and twisted it with a sick grin. I let out a scream of agony. "But you wanted my attention, and now you've got it."

"I hate you," I said, meaning it with every fiber of my being.

"I don't care. You're mine."

How sick could he be?

"I'm with someone else now." I wasn't sure why I was telling him that. "And he'll make you pay for this."

"We'll see about that."

The next thing I knew, Jeff's foot was coming toward my head. I flinched, but I wasn't fast enough to stop him. The toe of his boot connected with my temple, and darkness swallowed me whole.

TWENTY-THREE

TRAINER

"Are you going to place a bet?" Hawk asked, his notebook open in front of himself on the bar.

I was at The Blue Dog with Hawk, Swole, and Yoda to watch the UFC fight on the big flat screen. The place was full of people tossing back shots and getting geared up for what promised to be one hell of a fight.

"I'll put fifty on Hook to win with a knockout," I said, pulling out my wallet and tossing the bills onto the bar. Gabriel Hook was built like a tank and mean as hell. He was one of my favorite fighters.

Swole scoffed. "Hook's overconfident."

"For a reason," I said, nodding to the TV screen, which happened to be showing a series of clips from fights Hook had won.

"It's a weakness. Me, I'll always root for the underdog." She slapped two hundred-dollar bills on the table. "Snyder to win in three rounds."

I rolled my eyes. Tammy got pissed when Swole placed big bets and lost, but I wasn't going to say anything. It was her funeral.

I finished off the beer I'd been nursing for the past hour. It was warm, making it taste like piss, but I was purposefully going low on my alcohol intake tonight. I would be leaving right after the fight to go see my girl, and I didn't want to have to wait around to sober up enough to leave. I'd never get on my bike if I was too drunk to drive. I wasn't that big of an asshole.

The fight started, and everyone's attention went to the TV. There were people crowded around the bar, cheering as Hook took a strong lead in the fight. Snyder was up against the side of the cage with seconds, trying to protect his abdomen and face.

Suddenly, Swole straightened beside me, pulling her phone out of her pocket. I saw her frown before stepping away from the bar, going to the other side of the room, and answering the phone with her finger in one ear.

I went back to watching the fight, letting out a groan when Snyder brought a knee up to Hook's side. That looked like it hurt. The opponents made their way back to the center of the ring, circling each other...

"Come on," Swole said as she returned to my side. "We've got to go."

"But... the fight-"

"It's Erica."

I was off my barstool in less than a second. I followed Swole across the room and out the door of the bar.

"What about Erica?" I asked as we headed to our bikes. "What's going on?"

"That was Talia on the phone."

"Talia?"

"Her neighbor."

"Is that Las Balas asshole back to cooking?"

"No," she stopped and turned to me as we reached our

bikes, which happened to be parked side-by-side. "It sounds like Erica might be in real trouble. She said she heard yelling between Erica and a man, then her screaming."

Fuck.

I hopped on my bike without another word. My tires squealed as I peeled out of the parking lot with Swole right behind me. It had to be her husband. That bastard had found her somehow, and I wasn't there to protect her.

I tried not to think about why she didn't call me, but my mind couldn't be controlled in a moment like this. Was she hurt too badly to use the phone? Worse than hurt?

I couldn't stomach the thought.

When we reached Erica's house, Talia was standing on her half of the porch, smoking a cigarette. I barely spared her a glance as I opened the front door of Erica's home. It was unlocked.

I didn't have to look for her. She was laying on the living room floor less than ten feet in front of me.

"Fuck," I dropped to my knees beside her still body, eyes running over her. She was breathing, and I measured the steady up and down motion for a long moment. It made me feel marginally better, but the sight of swelling at her temple and a trail of dark red coming from her busted lip made my blood boil. "Baby, wake up."

I cupped her warm cheek, but there was no response. Looking up at Swole, I saw that she was on the phone. She gave Erica's address before hanging up.

"An ambulance will be here in five minutes."

"Good. Try to find Dominic."

Swole headed toward the stairs, but a voice spoke from the doorway.

"He's not here."

"How do you know that?" I asked Talia.

"I saw him leave. He ran out the back door with that dog by his side, going out the back gate. It was right before I heard Erica scream."

She looked shaken, but not nearly as much as I was.

"Listen, I had no idea what he was going to do to her. I would've called you guys before she got home if I'd known-"

"What the hell are you talking about?" Swole asked.

"The guy, the one that did this. I saw him breaking in through the back door a couple hours ago."

"And you didn't do anything?" I asked, enraged. She'd better not have been involved with this. I'd never hit a woman, but that didn't mean Swole couldn't.

"I was pissed, okay?" she said defensively, taking a long drag off her cigarette. "About you guys coming into my place and threatening me. So, I figured some guy burgling Erica's home was like karma or something."

A headache started to make my head throb. I took hold of Erica's hand, rubbing circles on the back with my thumb.

"But then I heard fighting and saw the little boy running away like the damn devil was chasing him. So, I called you."

"You're a real hero," I snarked.

"Hey, fuck you. I'm just trying to do the right thing here."

The ambulance pulled up in front of the house with its lights and siren on. Talia disappeared back into her half of the duplex as the paramedics came. I stepped back and watched as they checked her heart rate, breathing, and blood pressure.

The murmurings of the EMTs were barely audible over the sound of my heart beating in my ears. The sight of Erica's motionless body made me feel like I couldn't breathe. I noticed that her right foot was at an unnatural angle and stored that information away with everything else that had been done to her. Jeff would pay for it all. But first...

"I need you to get everyone together," I told Swole. She was technically above me in rank within Outlaw Souls, but this situation was personal, and it was only natural that I take the lead. "I want Dominic found."

"You going to the hospital?"

"Yes."

I rode behind the ambulance on the way to the hospital. I would have much rather been in the ambulance with her, and I had no problem lying about being family to get in there, but I knew that I wasn't likely to be at the hospital for long. I was going to join the search for Dominic as soon as I talked to the doctor.

Erica was wheeled through a set of swinging double doors that I was explicitly told I could not enter. I wasn't usually great at following orders, but the last thing I wanted was to get bounced by security. So I went straight to the waiting area, pacing the floor and trying not to glare at every nurse that looked my way. That would be misplaced anger.

Time seemed to be moving at a snail's pace as I waited to hear something about her condition. A cop showed up to take my statement, his beady eyes looking at me suspiciously as I told him that Erica was my girlfriend and I found her like that. I thought he might try to take me down to the station for further questioning, but instead, he told me not to leave town and that he'd be back later to get Erica's statement when she was awake.

"Mr. Lopez?" a doctor wearing deep blue scrubs asked as he approached me. I had told the nurses that I was Erica's fiancé so that they'd give me updates about her condition.

"Yes? How is she?"

"She'll be okay. Someone knocked her around pretty good, but there are few serious injuries. She has a couple of broken ribs, a twisted ankle, and probably a concussion."

"Is she awake?"

"Not yet. We've given her something for the pain and are waiting to see if she wakes up on her own."

"What if she doesn't wake up on her own?"

"We'll cross that bridge if we get there."

I didn't love the sound of that. "How long do you think she'll be out?"

"It is impossible to tell, but I'd say at least a couple hours."

Good. If possible, I wanted to find Dominic before then. I knew that she'd be worried sick about him if he wasn't there when she woke up.

"Can I see her?"

"Sure."

He led me to her room. She was the only person in there, in the bed hooked up to monitors. Bruising was starting to form on her face, and the swelling at her temple looked worse. She was dressed in a hospital gown, and the lower half of her body was covered with blankets, but I didn't need to see it to know where she'd been hurt.

I expected her to look fragile like this, but she didn't. Somehow, even in her unconscious state, I could see the fighter that I was crazy about. She was still so strong, and she'd get through this.

And it would *never* happen again.

There were two quick taps on the door before it was opened, and Tammy walked inside.

"Oh my god," her hand went to her mouth, and she crept closer to the bed until she was sitting in the chair at Erica's side. "Who did this?"

"Her husband."

"Husband? She never..."

"He's an abusive piece of shit, and she was hiding from him."

"That bastard," she sighed. "Swole sent me. Said you need to find Dominic? Is he okay?"

"I hope so. Stay with her. I'll be back as soon as possible. If she wakes up, call me."

"Got it. Swole said to meet her at the bar."

I felt like I was leaving behind a piece of my heart as I walked out of that hospital room, but Dominic had to be my priority. It wasn't just for Erica. I was worried about him too.

When I pulled into the parking lot of The Blue Dog, I was unexpectedly moved at the sight of my Outlaw Souls brothers and sisters already there, waiting to help me. I pulled up next to Ryder, who nodded in greeting. I got off my bike and spoke loudly to the assembled members.

"Thank you all for coming. We are looking for Dominic Mills." Getting out my phone, I pulled up a picture I'd taken of Dominic and Erica when they were staying at my place. Zooming in on his face, I held the phone up for everyone to see. "He might have a dog with him. He's my family, and I want him found safe."

As everyone mounted their bikes, I pulled Hawk aside. "I need a favor from you."

"What is it?"

"Go to Erica's house in case Dominic comes back there and use that time to do a little digging for me. I want to know where her husband is right now."

"Name?"

"Jeff Donovan."

"Alright, consider it done."

With that taken care of, I mounted my bike and joined the others in sweeping the streets of La Playa. He had better be okay. If something happened to that little boy, Jeff would pay for it, as well.

I HAD no idea where he could be. We had all been driving around for nearly an hour with no luck. Swole was with me, riding in traditional formation with me. I had a feeling that she might be keeping an eye on me, making sure that I was okay. Normally, I'd find that sort of thing annoying, but today, I felt like I needed it. I wasn't going to fall to pieces or any weak-ass thing like that, but I could easily get distracted by my overwhelming rage and frustration.

I pulled over onto the sidewalk in a residential area not far from Erica's house. It wasn't the best neighborhood, and I didn't think Dominic would come here for that reason, but I was getting desperate to find him. Swole pulled up beside me, pulling her helmet off her head.

"What's the plan?" she asked, sounding nearly as frustrated as I felt.

"I don't know," I said heatedly as I pulled my helmet off. "How am I going to go back to the hospital and tell Erica that I couldn't find her kid? *Fuck*."

I kind of wanted Swole to take the bait and snap back at me, but she was too smart to fall into that trap. Fighting with each other now would just be a distraction, and as much as I wanted one, it wouldn't do a damn thing to help this situation.

"You done?" Swole asked, raising one eyebrow. When I didn't respond, she just nodded. "Good. Now, try using your fucking head. You said the kid was family, lovely sentiment by the way, but now you have to prove it. Show that you know him. Where would he be?"

I scanned my brain. We weren't far from Erica's house right now. Dominic was on foot and hadn't been here long enough to have a ton of options.

Suddenly, an idea came to me, a memory really. The library was nearby. I could remember running into Erica outside the library. It was the place that I met Dominic for the first time.

"Follow me," I told Swole. When we were approaching the old brick building, I felt like I could collapse from relief.

There he was, sitting on the very bench that Erica and I had sat on together. The dog was lying at his feet while he kicked his legs back and forth.

I parked on the sidewalk in front of him, and he looked up at me. Swole stayed back in the street, but I could feel her eyes on me.

I was surprised when Dominic didn't come to me or even look happy to see me. I took a seat on the bench beside him and recognized that guilt in his eyes as it was a reflection of what I felt myself. Mine was because I'd let Erica down by not being there when she needed me most. But why did Dominic feel guilty?

"Hey, buddy," I said softly.

"Hi, Trainer." He turned his head to look the other way, hiding his face and the emotions that might be playing across it from me.

"Are you okay?" I asked, trying to scan his body for any injuries, but it was dark outside, and the streetlight didn't cast enough light for me to be sure.

He shook his head no, then his shoulders started shaking, and the muffled sound of crying reached my ear.

"Dominic," I placed a hand on his shoulder and carefully turned him so that he was facing me. As expected, there were tears streaming down his cheeks, and he was biting his bottom lip to try and suppress the sounds of his crying. Without another word, I pulled him into my chest, wrapping my arms around his tiny body.

I looked over at Swole, feeling helpless as I tried my damnedest to comfort this child. His weeping was tearing me up.

"It's okay," I said. "Your mom's okay."

He pulled away, looking at me in the face. "Is she really?"

Using the back of his hand, he wiped away snot from his nose. Dominic was an old soul, so that sometimes I forgot just how young he was. But at this moment, he was just a scared little boy.

"Yes, she's in the hospital, but she'll be okay. I promise."

"I-I'm so s-sorry," he said miserably.

"Sorry for what?" I asked, my brow furrowed.

"I left her all alone. I ran away."

Understanding dawned. "You were scared, right?"

He nodded. "And she told me to. I saw that he hurt her, but I didn't help. She told me to run away, and I did it."

"And you feel bad about that?" Of course, he did.

"I should've helped her," he sniffled.

"Listen," I placed my hands on his shoulders and made sure that he was looking into my eyes as I spoke. I wanted him to see the truth in my words. "You did the exact right thing. Your mom needed to know you were safe so that she could take care of herself, and it worked. She *is* hurt, but she's going to be okay. And that's because of you, bud."

"Really?" There was precious hope in his eyes.

"Yes. Now, would you like to go see her?"

"Can I? Right now?" he asked, almost smiling.

"As long as you're okay with riding on the back of the bike."

Dominic's eyes actually lit up with excitement, and I breathed a sigh of relief that his tears were gone. I hoped that Erica wouldn't mind that he was on a motorcycle. We'd never talked about that, but as far as I was concerned, these were special circumstances. At least I had Erica's helmet in my trunk box.

"Let's go see her," he said.

"I'll get the dog home," Swole said, picking up the furball as she pulled her cellphone out.

So, we left, heading to the woman that we both loved.

TWENTY-FOUR

ERICA

I awoke suddenly, with panic gripping my mind. My eyes popped open as I recalled what had happened and tried to figure out where I was, if I was okay.

Jeff. A threat. Danger.

Dominic. Gone. Safe.

Trainer. Staring at me.

The room around me was white, and my peripheral vision picked up machinery at my side, as well as raised bed rails. I was in a hospital.

Trainer was the only person in the room, sitting in a small plastic chair at my side that he was really too big for. His elbows rested on his knees, and he stared at me, nonplussed.

"Dominic?" I asked, my voice soft, but my body tense.

"He's here. In the bathroom," Trainer nodded toward a door on the other side of the room.

I relaxed, relief flooding me. I wasn't thrilled to be in the hospital, and Jeff having found me changed things, but at least I still had Dominic.

"He's okay?"

Before Trainer could answer, the bathroom door opened, and a blur of brown hair came flying at me.

"Mom, you're awake!"

Dominic had almost reached my bed when Trainer's arms shot out, snatching him up.

"Whoa, bud. Remember what we talked about? Your mom's injuries?"

"Oh. Right."

"What's going on?" I asked, starting to sit up. A sharp pain in my side put a stop to that quickly, and I gasped as I laid down flat once again.

"That," Trainer nodded. "Three broken ribs. A twisted ankle. Head injury. We talked about how important it was to be careful around you."

"Sorry," Dominic said. "I forgot."

"That's okay, honey," I told him. "Maybe you can sit next to me instead?"

Trainer placed him on the bed next to my hip. Reaching out, I ran a hand over his hair. He looked fine, completely unharmed.

"I wish you hadn't seen that," I said. He sobered up, and I could see the sadness in his eyes.

"I'm sorry, mom. I'm sorry I left. Trainer said it was good when he found me, but..."

"Trainer's right. You did great."

I looked at Trainer, and my heart seemed to expand in my chest. He had found Dominic. Nothing meant more to me in the world.

"Where is he?" I asked Trainer.

"I don't know yet. Your neighbor called Swole about the noise, and I found you unconscious on the floor. You were the only one in the house."

I didn't understand why Jeff would have just left me

like that, but I couldn't help feeling grateful to be alive. Jeff had shown himself to be a monster in the past, but today was different. He'd been out of control, more dangerous than ever.

I couldn't let him come back and hurt me again. Trainer would try to keep me safe, I had no doubt, but he couldn't be with me every minute of the day. As long as Jeff knew where to find me, I'd never be safe again. Everything I had here in La Playa, and the life that I'd built was collapsing.

I had to look away from Trainer as I thought about starting over somewhere else. Otherwise, I might burst into tears.

The doctor came in after that, checking my vitals. She lifted my blankets and checked my side, where my ribs were cracked, and the wrapping of my twisted ankle. I was told that I could have ice for my ribs, but the pain medication they were pumping in through my IV made it all a dull ache, as long as I didn't do anything to make my ribs protest too much.

Trainer's full attention was on me the whole time the doctor was looking me over, his intense gaze making it impossible to ignore his presence. I couldn't get a feel for what he was thinking, but I feared the worst. He'd barely spoken since I woke up, just answering my questions.

Was this too much for him?

He'd known about Jeff, but maybe finding me beaten unconscious made it all too real. I couldn't blame him if that was the case. Hadn't I known from the beginning that my baggage was probably a deal-breaker? It wasn't as if we'd been seeing each other for long. A couple of weeks of spending time together might not have been enough to convince him that I was worth this kind of hassle.

I tried to tell myself that it was a good thing. It would

make things easier when I disappeared again. I wouldn't be hurting him.

But it would break my own heart.

Trainer's phone rang right after the doctor left, and he excused himself to answer it, stepping out into the hall. The distance between us felt huge, and I hated it.

"Mom?" Dominic drew my attention away from Trainer, to where he was lying stretched out on a small black loveseat against the wall. "Is dad going to come back?"

"I don't know," I lied. I was sure that he would. Jeff wasn't the type to give up. He'd decided that he owned us.

"I don't want to leave," he said quietly. This kid was too damn perceptive.

The door of my room opened, and Trainer came back inside. He took a seat beside me once again, and this time he reached over, taking my hand.

"I have to go take care of some business," he said.

I knew that it was stupid to get upset about him leaving to take care of Outlaw Souls business, but there was an ache in my heart all the same. I was in the hospital, and I selfishly wanted him to stay at my side to comfort me.

But I wasn't going to ask him to. Maybe I was being stubborn, but I didn't want to make myself even more vulnerable than I already was only to be rejected. I had enough emotional turmoil to deal with right now.

"Tammy's going to come stay with you."

I looked at the clock on the wall. It was almost midnight.

"You know what? It's late, and I don't want Dominic to spend the night in a hospital. Maybe Tammy could just pick him up and take him back to her place for the night?"

Trainer hesitated. "But then you'd be alone."

Not if you stay.

"I need to sleep anyway," I said. I had a big day tomorrow, full of big decisions to make.

"Okay," he agreed. "I'll call her and make sure that's okay."

Tammy arrived fifteen minutes later. She came straight to my side, swooping down to give me a hug around my shoulders, so that she didn't hurt my ribs further.

"I'm so glad that you're okay," she said. "Is this why you wanted a fake ID?"

"What?" Trainer asked.

"I asked Tammy where to get a couple of fake IDs for Dominic and me," I explained. "I had hoped to stay in La Playa and wanted to solidify our identities here."

"I sent her to Hawk."

Trainer didn't say anything in response, but I knew him well enough by now to see that he was troubled. I couldn't figure out exactly why. Maybe he was upset that I asked Tammy instead of him?

"I better get Dominic home and in bed," Tammy said as he let out a huge yawn.

"Thanks, Tammy," I said sincerely. This was the hardest part about being a single parent, trying to make sure your kid was taken care of when something serious was going on, and you weren't able to yourself.

"It's no problem," she placed her hand on my shoulder and gave it a squeeze. "You're a part of the Outlaw Souls family now, and we take care of our own."

I wanted to believe that, but I wasn't like Tammy. She was *married* to Swole. They'd been together for years. I cared about them, and I was pretty sure that I loved Trainer, but that didn't matter if it only went one way.

Tammy left with Dominic, and Trainer stood from his

seat, lingering uncertainly. "I'll come back first thing in the morning," he promised.

Leaning down, he pressed a chaste kiss against my forehead before heading for the door. I wanted so much more. I wanted him to lay in this uncomfortable hospital bed with me in his arms and to tell me that everything would be okay, even though we both knew the threat of Jeff's unstable violence was still out there.

I watched him walk out the door. The second he was gone, the silence in the room felt suffocating. Even the machines at my bedside were silent. Reaching over the table next to me, I picked up three different remotes. The red one said the word *Nurse* and had a single button. Pretty self-explanatory.

The other two looked similar, but one was for the TV, and the other had a cord that was attached to my bed. I used the second one to raise the top of the bed into a sitting position, nice and slowly. My ribs throbbed, but I'd have to get used to that. The doctor had already told me that they would take about six weeks to heal. It was going to be difficult to move to a new place with this injury.

With that depressing thought, I carefully swung my legs over the side of the bed, hissing through my teeth. The pain medication wasn't strong enough to mask the effects of all this movement. I briefly considered calling a nurse, but I *needed* to be independent right now, to prove to myself that I could do it. Soon enough, I'd have no choice.

I held my breath as I lowered my feet to the floor. Forgetting to avoid putting weight on my injured ankle, I almost collapsed as pain engulfed me.

"Shit," I cried out.

A fresh wave of anger at Jeff gave me the strength to continue. So, I gripped my IV pole and used it as a crutch to avoid putting too much weight on the bad ankle. It seemed to take forever to get to the bathroom, but I eventually made it and felt a small sense of victory.

I wanted a shower to try and wash away this shitty day, but I didn't dare try to do that by myself yet. If I fell in there, I could end up in much worse condition. So, I used the toilet, then washed my hands and face. When I looked at myself in the mirror above the sink, I stilled, staring at my reflection. The bruises and swelling made me feel sick.

I looked like the battered wife that I was, and for some reason, the sight of it made me feel light-headed. This was my reality. I had known that for a long time, but seeing myself like this was different. It made me feel hopeless.

I just wanted to be free of Jeff.

But I knew that when I closed my eyes tonight, I'd see him in my nightmares. There was no true freedom. Maybe there never would be.

When I finally made my way back into the bed and under the covers, my entire body seemed to ache. I knew that I should sleep like I said I was going to, but I didn't want to relive the horror of what happened to me today. So, I picked up the TV remote instead.

It was almost an hour later that I fell into a restless sleep watching reruns of The Office.

TWENTY-FIVE
TRAINER

I hated leaving Erica alone in that cold hospital room. She didn't ask me to stay, or even why I was leaving, but I couldn't shake the feeling that she was disappointed.

I'd make it up to her.

For now, I needed to focus on making sure she was safe. When she spoke about obtaining fake IDs so that she could stay in La Playa, it didn't escape my notice that she was speaking in the past tense. She was already thinking about fleeing again.

That was unacceptable. I needed her and Dominic. There was no denying that they had both stolen my heart.

So, when Hawk came through with the location of her husband, I knew that I needed to go have a conversation with him tonight. He was staying at the Castle Motel right off the freeway. It was a low-budget, seedy place, which surprised me, since Erica had mentioned that the guy was loaded. My only guess was that he chose it to stay under the radar. That was how people like this worked. They knew how to get away with shit, which included staying at one of the few places in La Playa that still accepted cash and didn't exactly worry about checking identification.

Luckily, Hawk had connections just about everywhere, and that included this motel. I pulled into the parking lot, cutting the engine of my bike as I looked up at the second floor. Hawk's contact was a housekeeper that told him a man fitting Jeff's description was staying in room 223.

I sat on my bike for a moment, trying to decide how to handle this. I knew that finesse had never been my strong suit, so I followed my instincts. Going up the squeaky metal stairs to the second floor. I walked past a dozen doors before stopping in front of his room. Raising my fist, I pounded on his door with a thunderous boom. Once. Twice. Three times.

As soon as I heard the door unlatch, I lifted my booted foot and kicked the door open, knocking the man on the other side backward with a cry of surprise. He landed on his ass at the foot of his queen-sized bed. Stepping into the room, I slammed the door shut behind me.

"Jeff Donovan?" I asked. I'd never bothered to check out what the guy looked like before, so I wanted to be sure I had the right guy.

"Who the hell are you?"

He was struggling to his feet, and I let my eyes sweep the room. The man was wearing a pair of pajama pants, and I spotted his dirty clothes tossed carelessly on the floor by the TV stand.

"I said, who the hell are you?" the man repeated, sounding pissed. He kept his distance, though. He probably recognized that I had twenty pounds of muscle on him and a hell of a bad attitude.

I ignored him as I stepped over to the clothing and

grabbed his jeans. Sure enough, his wallet was still in the back pocket. I pulled it out.

"You're robbing me? Seriously?"

He must have been enraged at this idea, as he went charging at me. I swung out a fist, catching him across the face before he'd been close enough to lay a finger on me. He went down hard, and I took the opportunity to flip open the wallet. There was his smiling face staring up at me from his driver's license. It was him.

Jeff Donovan. Wife-abusing piece of shit.

He groaned from his spot on the floor, but it didn't take long before he was back up on his feet. *Good.* I wanted a fight.

"Who are you? What do you want?" he was getting angrier.

I could already see a purple bruise forming on his cheek where I'd hit him. It gave me more satisfaction than a decent man would get, but I didn't care. What I'd come here for was far from decent.

"I want retribution."

"What to hell are you talking about? I haven't done anything to you, man. I don't even know you."

Jeff didn't try to come at me again. I was bigger than him, taller and more muscular. He seemed to know instinctively that he couldn't overpower me like he did Erica. That thought brought my anger surging forth, and I closed the distance between us in two long strides. Remembering Erica's broken ribs, I balled up my fist and aimed for Jeff's side. He tried to back away, but I held him in place with one hand, my fingers digging into his shoulder as I jabbed him in the ribs three times in quick succession.

He let out a pathetic cry of pain and tried to push me away but ended up propelling himself backward until he crashed into his nightstand, where I noticed a line of coke waiting to be snorted.

"What the fuck?" he yelled, holding his side as he fumbled around for his cell phone that was also on the nightstand.

"If you're planning to call the cops, don't bother. They'll take forever to get to this side of town." I chuckled humorlessly. "I bet you thought you were pretty damn smart to stoop so low as staying in a place like this. No one would ever trace you here, even if your wife did end up in the hospital."

Jeff froze as realization flashed across his features, followed by hot anger.

"My wife? This is because of Eve?"

"Yes," I growled. "I'm here to show you what happens when you put your hands on her."

I shoved him backward into the wall, making him bump his head. His eyes looked glazed, which made me frown. No way was I going to let him pass out already.

The bump on the head must have rattled his brains because he tried to take a swing at my face. I caught his fist and forced the hand open. Deciding to *really* send a message, I bent back his index finger in one quick jerk. That could be payback for her ankle.

Jeff let out a scream, but I wasn't worried about anyone hearing and calling the cops. People stayed at this hotel because they had their own questionable shit going on, and no one wanted the La Playa PD poking around. At least Jeff looked fully awake now.

"What the fuck is wrong with you?" he shrieked as I went ahead and pocketed his phone, just in case he tried to call the cops again.

"You're going to leave town tonight. Go home. File for a

divorce. After the papers are sent to Erica... I mean, *Eve*, you will never have contact with her or Dominic again."

My tone left no room for negotiation. He'd do what I said, or I'd make him regret it. Jeff was cradling his hand to his chest, but I could still see a fire in his eyes.

"What goes on in a marriage is between a husband and wife."

I really hated that he kept referring to her as his wife. It wasn't just because I hated the reminder that she was still married to this ass, it was because of the tone he used, as if he was talking about a prized possession. He might think that Erica and Dominic belonged to him, but he was dead wrong. He'd blown his chance to have them in his life in any way. It was over.

"A marriage? Is that what you call this? She's trying to get the fuck away from you."

"Oh my god, are you fucking her?" he let out a laugh that was bordering on hysterical. "That clever bitch, shacking up with a damn pit bull that she can sic on me when she can't handle fighting her own battles."

This guy just didn't know when to quit. I shut him up with a right hook that crumpled his nose. He was on the floor again, and this time he didn't get up. He looked pretty well defeated, but I really wanted to drive the point home. Kneeling beside him, I shoved my face into his line of sight as he was holding his nose with his good hand.

"You heard what I said. Out of town. Divorce. Never return. If I ever see your face again, I guarantee you'll end up in the hospital. Got it?"

I stood up and waited a minute. When he just stared at me without a response, I kicked him in the side.

"Fine," he groaned, his pain-filled voice nasally. "Fine, I'll do what you say. Just leave."

"Gladly," I spat. Picking his wallet back up, I pulled out the handful of hundreds just to be an asshole. Then, I turned my back and headed for the door. I wanted to get back to Erica, but I should probably get a few hours of sleep first-

BANG!

My thoughts were cut off as the explosive sound of a gun going off sounded behind me, followed closely by the pain of a bullet grazing the top of my shoulder. *Holy shit.* The fucker was firing a gun at me.

Whipping around, I reacted without thought, embracing the instinct to protect myself. My gun was in my hand before I consciously decided to draw it. There was no time to assess Jeff since his next shot might not miss. It was him or me. I aimed for the largest part of his body, his chest, and put a slug into the middle of it.

My heart was hammering against my ribcage, and the adrenaline rushing through my body made my limbs shake. Jeff had been on his knees, holding a gun he pulled from his suitcase on the floor. When the bullet hit him, he stilled, looking down at the point of impact. Then, he fell forward onto the carpet, motionless.

I had killed him. It wasn't my plan. I had thought about it, of course, but I was too concerned about Erica's reaction. The guy treated her like crap, but he was the father of her child, and I assumed that she loved him once.

Would she hate me for this?

I hoped not. But, I couldn't keep it from her, I wasn't the type to do that. So, I'd find out how she felt soon enough.

Pulling my phone out of my pocket, I dialed Hawk's number.

"What's going on?" he answered in a sleepy voice. It

was almost two in the morning, so I wasn't surprised that he had been sleeping, but I needed his help.

"I need a clean-up crew," I said, tossing my gun down onto the bed. It would have to be tossed, but I could get a new one easily enough. I pulled out Jeff's cell phone too. That was something else that would need to be stopped.

"What?" Hawk sounded fully awake now. "Who's the vic?"

He must have a good idea of who it was already. He'd helped me find the guy.

"Erica's husband. We're in his hotel room."

"I thought you were just going to rough him up," Hawk said, but there was no accusation in his voice. This sort of thing happened, not often, but it was the reason we had these procedures in place. I could hear the unmistakable sounds of Hawk getting dressed on the other end on the line; the rustling of fabric, the drag of a zipper, and the jostling of the phone as he pulled on a shirt.

"Started out that way, but he pulled a piece on me, and I had no choice."

"Fuck. What a mess. You need medical?"

I reached up and touched my shoulder tentatively. It stung at the contact but wasn't too bad. I'd be okay I'd stitch it up myself later.

"No, I'm fine. Let's just get this taken care of."

"I'll be there in twenty."

While I waited for him, I took a seat on the edge of the bed. Shouldn't I feel something right now? Maybe guilt or happiness or something? I didn't have much of anything. The only strong emotion I had was concern about what Erica would say.

I'd been honest with Erica when I told her that I'd never

done this before. I'd been involved in some violent situations, but not killing. Not until now. But there was a comfort in knowing that she and Dominic were both safe because of my actions. That made it all worth it for me. Even if she hated me for it, I knew that I took care of her.

TWENTY-SIX
ERICA

"Stupid Jeff," I mumbled under my breath as I tried to get myself dressed. It was no easy feat, requiring a lot of bending and shifting that aggravated my injuries.

The doctor checked up on me first thing this morning, and I told her that I wanted to leave. She argued with me, saying that she was concerned about my head injury and wanted to keep me here for another day, but I insisted. I had barely established an identity here, and I didn't have health insurance. The thought of what this hospital stay might be costing me made my head spin. Besides, the sooner I started working on an exit strategy, the better.

I had managed to get my bra and panties on and was attempting to pull my jeans up my legs. They were a little tight around my bandaged ankle, and the act of bending down to get my legs in them was horrible for my ribs, but I managed. As I buttoned the pants, I automatically reached into my pocket for my cell phone, only to frown as I remembered that Jeff had crushed it.

I was without a phone, once again. So inconvenient. I

needed to find a ride home and call Tammy to arrange for Dominic to be brought to me.

There was a knock at the door. Before I could call out that I needed a minute, it opened. Trainer stepped inside, his eyes widening when he saw me shirtless. His gaze roamed over my bare skin on display, making a shiver run down my spine.

"What are you doing?" he asked gruffly. "Why are you getting dressed?"

"I'm getting released."

"Already? Are they sure you're okay?"

I shrugged. "*I'm* sure. I told the doctor I wanted to leave, so she's getting the discharge paperwork ready." I glanced at the clock. She'd left my room an hour ago. How long did it take to sign some papers releasing me?

Trainer crossed the room and picked up my t-shirt that was on the bed. There was a little blood on the front of it, I assumed from my busted lip, but I figured it would be okay until I got home. Then, I was going to throw all of these clothes away. I didn't need them around as a reminder of what happened.

"I can do it," I said, reaching for the shirt. I didn't want Trainer to help me. I didn't want myself to fall for him even more right now. Not if I was leaving soon.

But he shook his head firmly. There was no longer lust in his eyes. Instead, he was looking at my black and blue ribcage. He reached out a hand, as if to touch it, but stopped just short of his fingertips making contact.

"Can you call someone to give me a ride home?" I asked. "My phone's out of commission again."

"I've got the truck today," he said. "But I need to talk to you. If you want a ride from someone else after, I'll call Swole."

"Talk about what?" I asked as he helped me into my shirt. I had to admit that it was much easier not needing to lift my arms above my head, which made me feel like I was being stabbed in the lung.

"Take a seat," he insisted.

I got back onto the bed, sitting with my legs dangling over the side. "What's going on?"

Was this going to be when he told me that he was out? That this incident with Jeff was a deal-breaker?

Trainer took a deep breath, and I was shocked to realize that he was nervous. He also looked so tired, with big, dark circles under his eyes.

"Jeff's dead," he said.

Two words, that was it, but they changed my entire world. I felt like the universe was realigning, as I dared to hope that my struggle was finally over.

"What happened?" I asked.

"I didn't mean for it to happen. At least, it wasn't why I went over there..."

"*You* did it?" I asked, almost not believing it. He didn't seem capable of that to me.

"I had to. He had a gun. I went over there to talk to him," I could tell that was a lie based on his shifty eyes. I suspected that the "talking" had been pretty physical. "The second my back was turned, he took a shot at me."

I gasped. "Are you okay?"

He looked confused by my question, "Yeah. I was just grazed..."

I didn't like the idea of him being hurt at all, but I was glad to hear that he wasn't seriously injured. It could have been so much worse.

Jeff had a gun?

My stomach twisted, and I was glad that I had skipped breakfast. The man that beat the crap out of me had a weapon like that? I shuddered as I thought about what could have happened if he'd had it with him when he visited me yesterday.

"I'm so sorry." Trainer said earnestly.

"Are you going to go to jail?"

"No." He didn't offer any further explanation, but I could make an educated guess.

"Outlaw Souls?"

He nodded. "We take care of each other."

That was a little disturbing, but I tried to stay focused on the relief of knowing that Trainer wasn't going to be dragged away in handcuffs. I just didn't want to know what they'd done with the body or any of the details of covering it up.

I looked down at where my fingers were twisted together in my lap, trying to wrap my head around what Trainer was telling me.

"Are you mad?"

I looked back up into his eyes. Was I mad? Or sad, maybe?

I thought that I should be. I searched my heart for those feelings, trying to recall a time when I thought I loved Jeff, but I couldn't grasp that. Not anymore. All I could feel was relief. I was free of him. For the first time in nine years, Jeff wasn't a part of my life anymore. I didn't have to be afraid of him. Maybe it made me a monster, but I was glad he was gone.

"No," I said, reaching out and grasping Trainer's hands. I pulled him closer to me, and he didn't resist. "I'm not mad."

He didn't look like he believed me, so I put my arms

around him, ignoring the pulling around my ribs. I buried my face in his chest and let myself relax.

Trainer ran his fingers through my hair. I was always surprised by how gentle this big man could be.

"Do you regret it?" I asked.

"No," he replied without hesitation. "Maybe I should, but the way I see it, I was defending someone I love."

I lifted my head, looking up into his face. "Love?"

Trainer gave me a little half-smile as he looked at me warmly. "Of course. You didn't know?"

"Well, you've never said it..."

"Let me fix that," he placed his hands on each side of my face, his brown eyes shining with affection. "I love you, Erica."

"Eve," I said, wanting to hear him say it. "Call me Eve."

"I love you, Eve."

"I love you too."

Trainer placed a soft kiss against my lips, carefully avoiding the spot that Jeff had busted open.

It was hard to believe that I never had to fear him again, that I could stay here, living my life as normal, with my real name. I never would have asked him to do this, never would have thought it was something that I *wanted,* but Jeff had pushed me too far, and I wouldn't allow myself to grieve his loss. My dark past needed to stay behind me because the future was bright.

"EVE?" Tammy said, scrunching her nose. "Your name is Eve?"

"Yep," I confirmed. It had been a week since I left the hospital, and I was in Swole and Tammy's apartment on the ground floor of the Outlaw Souls complex. Our boys were in the next room, playing a video game. I wasn't a big daytime drinker, but when Tammy had offered to open a bottle of sweet red wine, I gladly accepted a glass.

I was still in the early stages of healing from my final altercation with Jeff. It had been a whirlwind of a week. Trainer had talked to Ryder and arranged for a larger apartment so that Dominic and I could move in with him. He offered to move into the duplex with me, but the place didn't feel the same to me after Jeff attacked me there. I knew he was gone, but the trauma he caused still lingered, transforming that place from a home to an empty shell with a very bad memory.

Here, I felt safe. We were surrounded by his fellow Outlaw Souls, and I knew that they would look out for me as they would for Trainer because we were so important to him. That was what Tammy meant when she said we were family.

Family was such a nice thing to have after everything we'd been through. Dominic and I had come to La Playa completely alone, but I found something that I hadn't even been looking for in Trainer.

"I don't know," Tammy said, "it's weird to think of you as anything other than Erica."

"You'll get used to it," I assured her. I, for one, was thrilled to be embracing my real identity. I even had an appointment with a hairdresser later in the week to have my hair returned to its natural color.

"I supposed I'll have to, since you're sticking around," she smiled. "You know, I was worried when I visited you in the hospital. I could see the fear in you, and I thought you were already planning to run away."

"I was," I admitted, after taking a long sip of my wine.

"Well, I guess it all worked out well, with that bastard husband of yours having that accident and all."

I wasn't sure if Tammy was speaking what she believed to be the truth or if she was just being delicate about the topic because our sons were nearby. I wasn't sure if Swole would have shared the truth with her. Either way, that *was* the official story. Jeff's body had been discovered in his mangled car in southern California. It looked like he'd been driving along a mountain road and ended up going over the edge, most likely due to the cocaine, since they'd found copious amounts in the car.

At least, that was what the police officer said when he showed up to break the news. The distance the car fell was so massive that his body had been badly damaged, and the cause of death was clear without an autopsy. That didn't sound quite right to me, but I suspected that someone might have been paid off to sweep this under the rug.

I wasn't sure how the Outlaw Souls pulled it off, but it did explain why Trainer seemed so tired the morning after his deadly altercation with Jeff. It was a long round trip drive down to the southern tip of the state.

"How's Dominic doing?"

"Wonderful," I said truthfully. I had told Dominic that his dad wouldn't be coming back. I'd been careful to avoid the word dead, but he was an exceptionally bright kid, and I thought that he had a pretty good idea anyway. "He and Trainer are getting along well."

"You know, I never would have pegged him as the father type, but he's really taken to it, hasn't he?"

"I've been thinking the same thing lately, but I don't know how he really feels about Dominic, you know?" Maybe the wine was a bad idea, as it seemed to be making me more loose-lipped than usual.

"You think he just accepts the kid because he loves you?"

I nodded, "It's what I'm afraid of. I want him to love Dominic, not just tolerate him because we're a package deal."

"Have you asked him about it?"

"Not yet. I feel like everything has been happening so quickly. I've barely had the chance to catch my breath."

Not only had Dominic and I moved in with Trainer, but I had to deal with Jeff's estate. As his wife, everything he had was now mine. The house, the money, everything. I didn't particularly want it. The money made me feel cheap somehow, like I was being paid off for my suffering. A lot of it was going to charity, with enough put aside to put Dominic through college. The problem with the house was the same problem I had with my duplex. It was tainted by the things Jeff had done to me there. So, I was selling it. Before it went on the market, I wanted to return one more time and see if there's anything I want to keep, since I had to leave so quickly when I came to La Playa. I had been delaying the return trip until Trainer could take time away from the club and his work on the latest bike he'd been fixing up. He didn't want me to go alone. Ever since finding me unconscious on the floor, he'd been in touch at all times. He even bought a Bluetooth headset that he had installed in his helmet so that he could take calls when on rides. He also rarely let me go anywhere alone without a fight. Some people might find it annoying, but I recognized it for what it was: uncontrollable fear. If he needed to be a little overbearing for a while to feel better, I was going to let him. Besides, it was nice having someone care so much. I wasn't sure what I did to deserve it.

"Find time to tell him about your concerns. It might be

difficult to find a good balance in the relationship at first, since you can't force an emotional attachment. But trust me, it's very possible to love a child that's not biologically related to you with all your heart."

I knew that she was right. There was no way to know what Trainer felt without asking him. I had already made the mistake of assuming that I knew what he was thinking when I woke up in the hospital. I wouldn't do that again.

My phone vibrated on the kitchen table, and I picked it up to see a message from Trainer.

Just got home. You with Tammy?

It was more than just a lucky guess. I wasn't able to work until my ribs healed – the ability to move around freely was obviously an important part of teaching yoga – so I had been spending a lot of time with Tammy during the day, since she only worked part-time at the fitness center. It gave me some much-needed adult company while Trainer was at the auto shop. I typed out a quick response.

Yep. Playdate for Dom and Emory.

I had barely sat my phone back down when it buzzed again. I gave Tammy an apologetic smile, but she was used to it by now. Frequent texting was a part of the extra-protective vibe he'd had lately. Opening up his message, I was surprised by what I saw.

Come to our place. Leave Dominic with Tammy.

Okay, that was weird. I checked with Tammy, and she was fine with looking after Dominic for a while. So, I climbed the stairs up to the second floor, where our new apartment was. When I opened the door, I didn't see Trainer anywhere. I walked through our empty living room, past the kitchen, and into the hallway that led to our bedrooms. I automatically headed to our bedroom, assuming that Trainer wanted to take full advantage of some time alone by breaking in our new bed, but as I passed Dominic's room, I saw that the door was ajar.

"Trainer?" I asked, pushing the door open the rest of the way and stepping into the bedroom.

"What do you think?" Trainer asked, holding his arms out. All around us, Dominic's room, which had been completely undecorated until now, was covered with insect-related posters. There was a comforter on his bed with pictures of moths and butterflies, and I spotted a new desk on the corner with a box that contained a bug collector kit. "Is it too much?"

My jaw dropped as I looked around, not sure what to say.

"You did all this for Dominic?" I asked, feeling choked up.

"Of course," he answered simply, as if it were no big deal. "He's nuts for bugs, and we hadn't gotten around to decorating in here yet, so I thought I'd surprise him. I ordered it all online, but once I set it up in here, I thought I might have gone overboard."

"I think it's amazing," I swallowed back my tears, but Trainer frowned as he noticed the raw emotion on my face.

"Hey," he stepped closer and took ahold of my hands. "What's wrong? How did I upset you?"

"You love him." It wasn't a question. I didn't need to ask anymore. Trainer was the kind of man whose actions spoke louder than his words.

"And... that makes you sad?"

"No," I said, slapping his chest playfully. "It makes me happier than I've ever been. I wasn't sure how you felt about taking on the responsibility of a kid."

"You and your doubts," he rolled his eyes, but didn't

look like he was really upset. "I'll tell you how I feel. I feel like he's mine. I *want* him to be mine."

"You do?" Damn it, the tears were back, and there was no stopping them this time.

"Yes, but I know I'll have to earn that position."

He was already more of a father to Dominic than Jeff had ever been. In my opinion, he'd more than earned the right to be Dominic's father, but I loved that Trainer wanted to try to win him over.

"Let's go get him, then," I said, "but you know that we're going to have to go to the park this weekend to test out that bug collecting kit."

"I'm counting on it," he said.

We left the apartment hand-in-hand. Life might not be perfect, but things were good. I finally had peace and a new life to spend with my man.

EPILOGUE: TRAINER

"Dominic, get your shoes on," I heard Eve call out. "I don't want to be late to go see Mama Tammy."

"Five more minutes," Dominic yelled back from his spot beside me.

I hid a smile. Ever since I talked Eve into letting him have the newest fighting game, he'd been hard to pry away from the PlayStation. As a parent, I knew I had to be disapproving, but I secretly liked it because he always wanted me to play with him.

"Dominic," Eve's voice called out again. She sounded pissed.

I nudged Dominic lightly in the side with my elbow. "Go get the shoes, bud."

He paused the game and let out a little sigh. "Why can't I just stay home and play?"

"Because Mama Tammy is expecting us. We can play more when we're all home again," I took the controller from his lax hand. "Now, scoot."

"Okay, dad."

That word came out of nowhere, and it froze me.

Dominic didn't seem to notice as he got up from the floor and headed to his room to get his shoes. I was still sitting in the middle of the living room floor, in front of the TV when Eve came out of our room, putting in a pair of earrings as she walked.

"Are you okay?" she asked, stopping beside me. I looked up at her, noting that she looked gorgeous in her emerald green wrap dress. It hugged her curves just right and complimented her flaming red hair.

"Yeah," I said, the word coming out high-pitched and soft. I cleared my throat and repeated myself, "Yeah."

"Okay... then what are you doing?"

I stood up, leaving the game console controllers where they lay. "You won't believe this," I said softly, so that Dominic wouldn't hear. I could hear the excitement in my voice. "Dominic just called me dad."

Eve's smile lit up her entire face. "Really?"

"Yeah," I confirmed. "Out of nowhere. Like it was no big deal."

"That's great, baby."

Eve hugged me tightly.

"Maybe we should postpone this trip," I said, earning a frown from her.

"Trainer, this isn't just a trip. It's our honeymoon, and it's already long overdue."

She was right, of course. We had been married for three weeks now, and postponing the honeymoon any longer wasn't a good idea. It was just that leaving Dominic behind right now felt wrong. We'd all been living together for six months, and he'd finally called me dad.

"He's not going to stop thinking of you as his dad just because we're gone for a week."

"You're right. I just feel like this is a big step forward in our relationship."

"It is, but it's a solid relationship. Don't worry so much."

"I'm ready," Dominic said, merging from the bedroom with his shoes on.

"Good. All the suitcases are in the car, including Dominic's," Eve told me.

She and Dominic got in the car, while I followed along on my bike. We were heading to Mama Tammy's place, like we did most Sunday afternoons, but this time Eve and I would be leaving after dinner to go on a ride to Las Vegas, where we'd be spending a week alone together. Gambling, shows, and as much time between the sheets as I could get. I loved Dominic like he was my own son, but I was well-aware of how having a kid around made it hard to find time for sex.

I planned to make up for any missed opportunities with my bride this week.

When we reached Mama Tammy's house, she opened the door on the second knock, while my fist was still in the air. As usual, she greeted Dominic first, sweeping him up into a bone-crushing hug. She always said that Dominic was the closest thing she'd ever have to a grandchild, so she was going to spoil him.

Next, Eve and I got kisses on our cheeks. The three of us entered the house, and I immediately recognized the meal we were having by smell alone.

"Tuna casserole again?" I asked, pouting at Mama Tammy. We'd had that as least once a month since Eve and Dominic started coming to these weekly gatherings.

"It's Dominic's favorite," Mama Tammy replied dismissively.

"Trust me, I know. Maybe you could make *my* favorite sometime instead."

"Boy, you've gotten spoiled since you met this one," she said, gesturing to Eve. "You get homemade meals every night, and all of a sudden, you start sassing me."

I rolled my eyes, but I couldn't help smiling.

It was funny when I was young, I always thought of myself as someone with no family. I had tried to accept it, but it was hard. I felt like I was missing something. Then Mama Tammy came along. Now, I had Eve and Dominic. They might not be blood, but they were the family I chose, and I couldn't be happier.

We sat down at the table together, falling into easy conversation as we filled each other in on everything going on in our lives.

"We really appreciate you watching Dominic while we're gone," Eve said.

"Oh, please. It's a pleasure. It's been too long since I had little kids in this house. I loved taking in foster children. It was the great joy of my life."

"You're a good woman," Eve said.

"It's easy to love kids."

I looked over at Dominic. I had to agree.

"So, are you planning to have more?"

Mama Tammy's question took me off-guard. I whipped my head around, looking at first her, then Eve. She looked just as surprised as I was. We'd never talked about it.

"Uh... I don't know," I said.

The atmosphere at the table got awkward. We all focused on our food for several minutes, not meeting each other's eyes. Mama Tammy leaned over toward Dominic and spoke with a stage-whisper, "Did I touch a nerve or what?"

Dominic just shrugged.

"We just haven't talked about it," I said. But now that the idea was in my mind, I couldn't deny that it was compelling. I wanted to see Eve pregnant with my child, to be there to hold the baby right after it was born. I wanted to be a better parent than both of mine combined.

"If you do it, I want a brother," Dominic said. "Girls don't like bugs."

Everyone at the table chuckled.

"We don't get to choose the sex of the baby," Eve explained, "but if it's a girl, you can still teach her all about bugs."

"So... you're going to do it? Are you going to have a baby?" Dominic's smile broadly.

Mama Tammy looked at Eve and me with both her eyebrows raised in a silent question.

I looked at Eve. We were being put on the spot here, but as our eyes met, that didn't seem to matter. I could see the answer written on her face, and it was the same as my own.

"Yeah," I nodded. "I think we are."

Dominic cheered while I put my arm around the back of Eve's chair, and she rested her head on my shoulder. Mama Tammy stood.

"I think that calls for some dessert," she said. "Come along, Dominic. Help your Mama Tammy."

When Eve and I were alone in the room, I tilted her chin up so that she was looking at me. "Are we really going to do this?" I asked. "Do you want it?"

"I do. You know, I decided a long time ago that I wasn't going to have any more. It was hard enough to keep Dominic safe. I didn't want to bring anyone else into my messy life, as it wouldn't be fair to the child. But now, it doesn't seem like that. Now, a child would be a blessing, coming into a good life."

"You know I'll do whatever I have to do to keep you all safe, right?"

"Of course."

We left Mama Tammy's house after eating dessert. It was hard to leave Dominic behind, but we knew that he'd be well taken care of. I straddled my motorcycle and waited for Eve to get on the back.

She'd gotten much more comfortable back there and had even gone a few rides with the Outlaw Souls. We finally got to take the big ride to Utah that I had been planning, but Eve didn't tag along for that one.

Still, it was a good trip. The club would always be like my second family, and organizing these rides would always be my passion.

Now, I fired up the Harley and pointed it east. This might end up being my favorite ride yet. Because I loved to ride, and I loved Eve.

WHAT'S NEXT?

Turn the page to find out where it all began for The Outlaw Souls MC and **grab your FREE copy of The Prequel**! I'll also give you a sneak peak into the in the next book in the series, *Colt*!

GET YOUR FREE BOOK!

Hey hey!
*Get your **FREE copy of Outlaw Souls: The Prequel** sent directly to your inbox. You'll also be the first to hear about upcoming new releases, giveaways, cover reveals, chapter reveals, and much more.*

CLICK HERE To Get Your Free Book

BLADE

You don't want to miss the rest of the **Outlaw Souls series**! If you enjoyed *TRAINER* check out my next book of the series called *BLADE*.

CLICK HERE To Read *BLADE* Now!

***BLADE* Book Blurb:**

There's a fine line between love and hate.

Blade came into my life like a wrecking ball. Tearing down my walls and rocking my world. Then I found out he was a member of Outlaw Souls. That was a problem, since my loyalty was to their enemy, Las Balas. My connection to them was one of blood, through my father and brother. I couldn't turn my back on that, no matter how much I wanted Blade.

Meanwhile, there was a new kind of trouble brewing in La Playa. Both of the rival clubs got caught up in the mess, which left me choosing sides. Sleeping with the enemy was addicting, but what about my family? It was time to make a real choice. Because things were heating up between Las Balas and Outlaw Souls, and it was dangerous to get caught in the crossfire.

Blade and I were meant to be enemies. Could we find a way to get past that and become so much more?

Click here to find out for yourself. Happy reading!

1. KAT

I froze in place as I stepped out the front door of my house and saw that my front tire was flat as a pancake.

"No, no, no," I groaned, hurrying forward to get a closer look as if I could possibly be mistaken.

No luck. It was flat, and I had to deal with it.

"Shit," I hissed under my breath as I threw my purse into the driver's seat and popped the trunk. I was going to kill my brother, Jason. He'd borrowed my car yesterday, and now my perfectly good tire was flat. No way that was a coincidence.

Grabbing the jack, lug wrench, and a spare tire out of the trunk, I hauled them over to the deflated tire. Taking a closer look, I spotted the problem. A nail was stuck in the rubber. I sighed and checked the time on my phone.

There was no way I was going to make it to work on time. *Damn it.*

Firing off a quick text to the owner of the tattoo shop where I worked, I tucked the phone into my back pocket and got to work. Luckily, my dad had taken the time to teach me how to change a tire back when I got my driver's license. It was one of the few bonding experiences we ever had. He said that being a girl was no excuse to not have basic knowledge about your car. So, I knew how to change tires and oil, replace spark plugs, and change the light bulbs in my headlights. I was no mechanic, but at least I felt somewhat independent.

I went through the steps as quickly as I could—loosening the lug nuts, lifting the car with the jack, and taking the flat tire off. I tossed it onto my front porch. Jason didn't know it yet, but he was going to buy me a new one. I put the spare in place and wrapped up the process. It only took about twenty minutes, but I wasn't much of a morning person and was barely going to make it to work on time before this. Now, I was officially behind schedule.

I drove like a bat out of hell through downtown La Playa, weaving in and out of traffic as well as I could on a busy Monday morning. I ignored the dinging of text messages coming through on my phone, knowing it was probably my best friend, wondering where I was.

I dug around blindly in my purse as I kept my eyes on the road. Finally, I felt the unmistakable shape of the pack of gum I stashed there. Pulling the Juicy Fruit out, I unwrapped it, tossing the wrapper onto the floor of the passenger side where it joined a dozen others and empty cans of various energy drinks.

I needed to clean out the car again. It was crazy how quickly it got trashed.

I popped the gum into my mouth, chopping away as the sweet, fruity flavor exploded on my tongue. Pulling into the parking lot of Ink Envy, I took the first parking spot I saw. The shop was a small white building on a corner lot. There was a mural painted along the side of the building, perfectly positioned to catch the eye of drivers along Blackburn

Drive. The owner had paid a graffiti artist to create an enticing image. He went with a woman holding a tattoo gun. Coming out of the gun was a rainbow of color that morphed into shapes and images. From left to right, it went from bright and vibrant to dark and striking. It was beautiful, and I still found myself staring at it in awe after working here for nearly three years.

But there was no time to stop and stare today. Locking up my car, I jogged over to the front door of the place, my Chucks eating up distance. I pulled open the door and took two steps before colliding with a tall man's hard body. I went reeling backward with a gasp as the man fumbled with the box in his hands, barely avoiding dropping it onto the linoleum floor.

"Oh, crap. Sorry, Gary," I said as I realized that I had run straight into my coworker. Gary had started working at the shop just a couple of months after I did. He was a talented artist, but not the most reliable person.

Not that I had room to talk on a day that I showed up so late.

"Whatever," he snapped. Brushing past me where I stood in the doorway, he stalked out the door without looking back. I furrowed my brow in confusion.

"What the hell was his problem?" I asked out loud, talking to myself. I was surprised to hear an answer coming from behind me.

"He was just fired."

I turned to see my boss, the owner of the shop, sitting behind the counter to the right side of the room. Brie liked to man the counter herself instead of hiring someone. It made her the face of the business for customers, the first person they would see when walking through the door. We were in a reception area, where the customers checked in and paid. No one was around, so we could speak freely.

"What happened?" I asked, shocked. Gary wasn't a close friend, not like the other tattoo artist, Piper, who was probably my best friend, but I saw the guy every day. He was a part of my world, and it was jarring to think that he was suddenly gone.

"The guy's a cokehead," Brie said, her voice dripping with disapproval. "I suspected it forever, but his work was good. I was willing to give him the benefit of the doubt until I was refilling supplies this morning and found his stash."

I winced. That was a big no-no.

"Yeah," Brie nodded, reading my oh-shit expression. "He brought that crap into *my* place. He's got balls of steel."

I laughed despite the seriousness of the situation. Brie didn't play around with that stuff. We were sub-contractors, but she was quick to remind us that this was *her* house. She didn't want to get a bad reputation, and drug use by the staff was a quick way to do that.

"Laugh it up, chuckles. You know this leaves us short-handed, right?"

That sobered me up. She had a point. Brie could do tattoos, but her time was usually spent doing other things. She was the only one that did piercings, for instance. That meant that Piper and I were the only full-time tattoo artists. My plate was already full on most days. Piper and I taking over Gary's workload was going to be rough.

"You going to hire someone else?" I asked as I started to make my way to the back of the shop. The area was divided into three sections by a half-wall. We all had curtains hanging from tracks on the ceiling that we could close if a client was getting a tattoo on a private area of their body.

"As soon as possible," she replied. I was almost out of sight when she called out, "Kat?"

"Yeah?" I turned.

"If you still want that piercing, we'll do it before we leave at the end of the day."

I smiled. "Perfect."

Walking into my workspace, I shoved my purse into a cabinet before taking a seat on a stool. I had framed examples of tattoos I'd done up on the wall, as well as a book of basic designs sitting on the counter. It had everything from butterflies to skulls and was useful for people that came in without a concrete idea of what they wanted, which wasn't common.

"Nice of you to show up," Piper said from the workstation beside me. There was a man in her chair, staring at his phone while she tattooed a panther onto his shoulder.

"It's Jason's fault. He gave me my car back with a damn nail in the tire. I had to change it out this morning."

"Why did he borrow your car, anyway?" she asked without looking up.

"Because all he has is a bike, and it was raining yesterday. I don't know where he needed to go, but he just kept whining about getting soaked until I gave in."

"You softie."

I chuckled. That might be the first time I was ever called that.

Picking up my trash can, I spit out the gum, which had already lost its flavor. I only chewed it as a deterrent, anyway, trying to kick my stress-induced smoking habit. I knew that cigarettes were terrible for my health, but it was a bad habit that I had picked up as a teenager. I usually only had one or two a day, but I had been attempting to quit for the last month. No more smelling like an ashtray for me.

Brie brought back my first client of the day, a woman I had been working with for the last couple of days. She had come to me to design a massive piece for her entire back. It was a flowering tree, its roots stretched along the base of her spine while the top branches spanned her shoulder blades. Yesterday, I had spent hours outlining the tattoo. Today, we were adding color.

As the client settled into place on my chair with her shirt off, I adjusted the height on my stool until I was comfortable and got to work. The buzzing of my tattoo gun was the only sound in my ears as I lost myself in the work.

I loved when the rest of the world fell away, and I could just create another masterpiece. Some people might not be too impressed with my profession, but I was happy. I considered myself an artist. My canvas was the human body, and my art lasted nearly forever.

My client was a champ, lying still and not even asking for a break. The only time I got a reaction out of her at all was when I was coloring in green leaves along her ribs. She tensed ever so slightly and sucked in a sharp breath.

I couldn't blame her for that. I had a tatt along the front of my right ribcage—the words *One Life To Live*—so I knew that it was one of the more painful areas to have tattooed.

After three hours, her tattoo was finished, and I snapped a picture of it for my portfolio. I had heard Piper take a couple of Gary's clients while I was working, so I knew that I was going to have to do the same. Taking a break before Brie had a chance to bring someone back for me to work on, I stepped out the back door and popped another piece of gum in my mouth. Pulling out my phone, I fired off a quick text to my brother.

Hey, asshole. You owe me a new tire.

I smirked as I sent it, knowing full well that he was going to try to squirm out of buying it.

Ten minutes passed quickly, and it was time to get back to work. Sure enough, when I stepped inside, Brie was waiting for me with a skinny man that I'd never seen before. I had to try to squeeze him in before my one o'clock appointment. I hated being under pressure like that.

Brie had better find a replacement for Gary soon.

At the end of the day, which was an hour later than usual, I was more than ready for it to be over. I put the finishing touches on a pink hibiscus flower, wiping the ankle tattoo clean as the woman shook with tears in her eyes.

Some people just couldn't handle any amount of pain. They really had no business getting tattoos, but that wasn't my problem. The ones with low pain tolerances had money that was just as green as everyone else's. The only time it bothered me was when the customer kept asking for breaks, and the appointment ran too long.

Putting down my gun, I massaged my aching hand, flexing my fingers.

"Hell of a day, huh?" Piper had already cleaned her tattoo gun and was now sweeping the floor.

"Yeah. I could use a drink. You want to come?" I asked, starting my own cleaning process.

"Where do you want to go?"

I shrugged. "Anywhere but The Pit."

"Come on," Piper whined, leaning against the half wall that separated us. "Xander will be there."

"Yeah, along with all the other Las Balas members. Including my dad."

I did *not* party with my old man. We weren't that close, but I didn't want him to see me tossing back tequila shots or shaking my ass on the dancefloor. It would be weird. My dad was at The Pit nearly every night since it was the hangout of his motorcycle club. Xander was a part of the club, too, and nearly ten years older than Piper. I didn't get the attraction, but I was never into older men. I wasn't going to be a twenty-three-year-old trophy wife. If I ever settled down at all, it would be with someone that was young enough to have some fun and keep up with me in the bedroom.

"Let's go to that place by the beach," I suggested.

"The Copper Bar? I guess that'll be okay. They have daiquiris for two dollars tonight."

"You ladies going out on a Monday night?" Brie asked as she walked through the curtain that divided the front of the shop from the back. "Oh, to be young again."

"Come with us," I said as I took a seat on my stool. Brie was carrying the piercing gun, so I gathered my hair over my right shoulder and tilted my head.

"Please," she rolled her eyes. "If I went out drinking tonight, there's no way I'd be able to drag my happy ass out of bed in the morning."

She chuckled while disinfecting my skin for a tragus piercing. The little piece of cartilage that jutted out over the ear canal was supposed to be one of the most painful piercings you could get, but I didn't mind a little pain. It was all temporary, and, in the end, I reaped the rewards. This time, I was going to have a cute piercing with a dark blue stud that complimented the aquamarine one in my nose.

"You should come," Piper chimed in. "You never know. You might meet a man."

"Oh, now *that's* tempting." Her voice was dripping with sarcasm. I couldn't blame her. Brie had been divorced an astounding four times and vowed that it would never happen again. "Ready, Kat?"

"Go for it."

I sucked in a deep breath as she counted down.

"Three...two...one."

I heard the clicking of the gun just as a stinging pain made me clench my teeth. Then, it was done. I knew it would ache for a while. This particular piercing took a long time to heal.

"You're set. You know the drill. Keep it clean and all that," Brie advised as I checked out the piercing in the mirror.

"Thanks, Brie. You ready for those drinks?" I asked Piper.

"Let's do it."

We left the shop together, getting into my car and heading for the beach. After a long day at work, I was ready for a good time.

2. BLADE

"Are you sure about this?" Alex asked as I wrapped the gauze around my hand, covering from the wrist to the knuckles.

"Absolutely," I said, finishing up one hand by applying tape and starting on the other. Behind me, I could hear the jeering and shouting of the crowd surrounding the fight circle, while the two men inside were silent, aside from the dull thud that resulted from their blows to each other's bodies.

"But the odds are four to one against you."

"I know," I smirked. "So, you're going to go put five hundred dollars on me to win."

"What?" Alex's looked at me like I was crazy.

I sighed. He'd always been like this, a voice of reason, as he liked to call it. Personally, I thought he needed to let loose a little, but it just wasn't in his nature. Sometimes it drove me nuts, but he was family, so I put up with it. And I'd never tell him, but there were times when he was the voice in my head, talking me down from being too reckless.

"Here." I pulled out the bills that had been rolled up in

my pocket, held together by a rubber band. "Put that down now, before my fight starts. We'll combine the winnings with my payment from the boss and walk out of here twenty-five hundred dollars richer."

"You sound pretty damn sure of yourself."

"I am." I had to be. If I walked into that circle, facing a monster of a man with at least thirty pounds on me, with anything less than full confidence, then I would be doomed before we even began.

Besides, I had no interest in walking away from here a loser.

"Fine, but don't expect me to push your wheelchair around when The Beast is done with you."

"Thanks for your pep talk," I called out after him as he stalked away to place the bet. "Your faith in me helps me to have faith in myself."

The only response I got was the middle finger thrown over his shoulder, which made me break out into loud laughter. It was perfect, just what I needed to cut through the tension before the fight.

I was new to street fighting, so this was only my third time here. My friend, Rick, had told me about the gig. He had been coming here for months, making decent money and, more importantly, working out some aggression. That was the main reason I kept coming. Sure, the money was nice, but I was more interested in working out my issues with my fists. I thought of it as nontraditional therapy. It was a hell of a lot better than nothing.

Rick had to work tonight, so I asked my cousin to tag along instead. The one thing I knew for sure was it was best not to come alone. Each win paid out a thousand bucks, and it wouldn't be out of the question for someone alone to be jumped by some of the men around here to get the cash.

The current fight ended, so I got to my feet. I did a few quick stretches, ending with cracking my neck. Despite my lack of street fighting experience, I was no stranger to a fight. As the only son of an army general, I was pushed to join up my entire life. My father even went so far as to insist that I attend military school and receive hand-to-hand combat training as a teenager.

I didn't know if he thought that would somehow motivate me to follow in his footsteps, but it didn't work. I hated the strict structure and emphasis on discipline. My father wasn't happy, and I didn't think our relationship ever recovered, but I decided quickly that I wasn't soldier material. It didn't take long to get kicked out of the place, but I had picked up some fighting skills by then. Over the years, I'd honed those skills in bar fights and a general knack for finding trouble.

"You ready?" Alex asked as he returned.

I just nodded before turning and starting to make my way through the crowd. They parted for me, many of them shouting taunting insults until I reached the edge of the circle, the boundary of which was marked with white spray paint on the concrete floor.

This warehouse was one of many old and abandoned ones on this side of town. The windows were boarded up, and the only entrance was a sliding metal door at the back of the building that had previously been a loading area for large trucks. It helped the guys running this place to keep track of who came and went, but it also meant there wasn't an easy getaway if we were ever busted. So, I hoped it never came to that.

On the other side of the crudely drawn barrier, I saw my opponent, a man that had earned the nickname The Beast with both his size and manner, stepping through the crowd on the other side. I could feel the buzz of anticipation in the air as the crowd got worked up for the fight. I knew that we were the main event of the evening. The new guy who was making a name for himself around here versus a man that was known for being big and mean. He wasn't undefeated, but he didn't lose often, either. I took his measure from twenty feet away.

The Beast wasn't much taller than me, but I had to admit that he was bigger. It wasn't all muscle, either. The two of us were both shirtless, and I could see that he was carrying extra weight around his middle. That could work to his advantage if he got me pinned beneath him.

Despite his extra weight, his shoulders were broad, and it was clear he didn't skip arm day at the gym. There was no doubt that he was strong. I was sure to get pummeled if he got his hands on me.

So, I had to make sure that didn't happen.

"Ladies and gentlemen," a voice rang out from my left. Turning, I saw the man in charge, Luca Bianchi, shouting to be heard above the crowd. "We've come to our last fight of the evening. Place your bets now. Will it be the up and coming biker, Blade?"

There was a smattering of hoots and cheers, but not much. It was a good thing I didn't care about that. It worked to my advantage to be underestimated.

"Or will it be the meanest son of a bitch I know, The Beast?"

This response from the crowd was much more impressive, and the idiot loved it. Throwing his hands into the air, he stepped into the middle of the ring, gesturing for them to cheer louder for him as if their support mattered at all.

It didn't. All that mattered was who was better in the ring. Tonight that would be me.

I was strong, with six-pack abs and my own sculpted biceps, but what would give me the edge in this fight was my speed. While The Beast was busy working the crowd, I stepped into the ring and circled around him. I stayed on the balls of my feet, making sure that I was at his back as he moved, just waiting for the signal to begin.

Finally, a shrill whistle cut through the air, and I ran forward, reaching my opponent before he even had a chance to figure out where I'd gone. A quick jab to the kidney made him let out a whoosh of air, but I was gone before he could react, facing him on the other side of our circle.

Most of the crowd around us booed, and I couldn't keep the smirk off my face. A lot of assholes were about to lose the money they bet against me.

The Beast let out a noise that I could only describe as a growl, his face turning red as he moved toward me. Anger was going to be his weakness. I moved out of his path quickly, landing a kick to the side of his knee as I went. His leg buckled, but he managed to straighten it out and stay on his feet.

A small part of me was glad that he didn't go down easy. I wanted a challenging fight.

I could sense the moment that The Beast started taking me seriously. When his eyes met mine again, the anger was still there, but I could also see a calculating look. He didn't move without thinking again.

Good. Now we could really begin.

The sounds of the crowd around us faded into the background as I became laser-focused on the huge man in front of me. Time dragged on as the fight got more intense. The only rule here was no weapons, so there was nothing that was off-limits.

I stuck to my strategy of quick jabs while staying out of reach, but The Beast had a long reach and was able to land a few blows. I had a couple of bruised ribs and a busted lip, but it wasn't going to slow me down.

The longer the fight went on, the more I tapped into my inner darkness, the anger and guilt that I had carried with me for ten years. It fueled me, making me more vicious. I barely felt the pain of the hits I had taken, and I got more daring, able to land several blows to the man's face. I even broke his nose.

Then, he got a hold of me. I knew that it might happen, and all I could do was hope that I'd inflicted enough damage to take him down. I took blows to my sides, trying to block them as well as I could with my arms, but it was the right hook to the temple that sent me reeling. I saw stars.

Stumbling back two steps, I couldn't get away from him, so I tapped into every ounce of aggression that I had. Bringing my arms up, I blocked his next blow. It brought him even further into my space, and, reacting on instinct, I brought my elbow across his face with all my strength. He was dazed, so I swiped his legs. It hurt my own shin, but he went down. Hard.

The sound of him hitting the concrete was a dull thud, and he didn't get back up. I stood over him, my chest heaving as I wiped blood away from my chin.

I barely registered the surprised reaction of the people around me as I walked out of the ring. Alex was at my side, and he wordlessly handed me a bottle of beer. I took a swig, savoring the cold liquid as it slid down my throat.

"Are you okay?" Alex was eyeing my lip, and I wondered just how bad it looked.

"I'll live."

"And you're lucky for that. That guy was a monster."

"I think he prefers to be called a beast."

"How can you make jokes after such a brutal fight?"

I shrugged. The truth was, I felt great. My adrenaline was still pumping, and I had let out some of my ever-present anger. Street fighting was a hell of an outlet.

"Let's pick up my money and head to the Blue Dog," I said. "I could use about five more of these."

I held up the beer bottle, then took another big swallow.

Alex didn't say anything else about the fight, but I knew that he had something on his mind. Everyone was starting to leave, with the few winners making their way to Luca's man, Gino, who handled the betting. I went to Luca first, collecting my winnings.

"I gotta say, you surprised me out there," he said while chewing on a toothpick and counting out my payment in twenty-dollar bills. "I can count on one hand the number of times someone has taken down The Beast."

"Yeah, well, don't be afraid to take a chance on the underdog next time," I advised.

I only got a grunt in response. Alex and I collected the money we won, and I pulled my black t-shirt back on, as well as my black leather jacket. Then, I tossed my empty beer bottle in a trash barrel on my way out the door.

The night air was crisp, as it had gotten colder when the sun went down. It was springtime, and the trees were just starting to get their leaves back.

"You wanna tell me what's on your mind?" I asked as we got into Alex's pickup truck. It was one of the nicest vehicles in the parking lot.

Alex worked as the foreman for a commercial construction company in nearby Trotter Beach, so he made good money, and it showed in his choice of vehicle. He was lucky no one broke into the thing in this neighborhood.

"Why are you doing this?" he asked, looking at me with tired eyes.

"The fighting?"

I leaned back against the leather seat and felt my aching ribs. They hurt, but I was pretty sure none of them were cracked.

"Yes, the fighting," Alex responded impatiently. "Don't you see how dangerous this shit is? What if the big bastard had knocked you down, fracturing your skull on the concrete? Do you think your friends in there would have called an ambulance for you?"

No.

"I don't have friends in there." I shot him a smile. "That's why I brought you."

He didn't look amused. "Yeah, well, it's a one and done for me. I know you're really fighting your own demons, but there's got to be a healthier way to do that."

I shook my head and looked out the window. There was a long moment of silence between us, but I eventually broke it.

"What the hell would you have me do? Go to some headshrinker?"

The idea was laughable. I wasn't the sharing type, especially with some stranger. The fighting worked for me. I didn't need to talk about my damn feelings.

"I think they prefer the term therapist."

Alex pulled into the parking lot of the Blue Dog, and I was eager to get inside the bar. Even this conversation with Alex hadn't brought me down from the high of winning, and I wanted to enjoy it. The Outlaw Souls were inside, and as a prospective member of the motorcycle club, I belonged among them. I stepped out of the truck, but when I turned to close the door, I saw that Alex hadn't moved.

"You're not coming?"

He shook his head. "I'm not in the mood tonight. Get one of your biker friends to give you a ride home."

I shut the door of his truck, and Alex left before I even made it across the parking lot. I knew he wasn't happy with me, but he'd get over it. I was sure he'd come again if I needed him to have my back. So, I brushed off his concerns and walked into the bar, where I could start spending my winnings.

CLICK HERE To Continue

CONNECT WITH HOPE STONE

Come hang out with the most amazing group of "Stoners" and join in on all the fun! This is an exclusive group where readers and fans of drama-filled, steamy romances come together to talk about Hope's books. This is the place to engage with other fans in a fun and inclusive way as well as get access to exclusive content, find out about new releases, giveaways, and contests, as well as vote on covers before anyone else and so much more!

CLICK HERE to join the Hope Stone Readers Group on Facebook.

ABOUT THE AUTHOR

Hope Stone is a contemporary romance author who loves writing hot and steamy, but also emotion-filled stories with twists and turns that keep readers guessing. Hope's books revolve around possessive alpha men who love protecting their sexy and sassy heroines. But enough of the boring stuff. **How about we kick it up a notch because...**

The fun stuff, the juicy stuff, the REAL stuff is in the Facebook group! It's a judgement-free, safe and fun group where romance lovers can be themselves and the primary spot for me to let my freak flag fly!

WARNING: *If you're not a fan of laughing your ass off, seeing ridiculously hot biker dudes on the daily, or getting exclusive freebies then this group might not be for you.*

CLICK HERE to join the Hope Stone Readers Group on Facebook.

Printed in Great Britain
by Amazon